MW01505795

The
Angels Talk

The Angels Talk

*

How to Find
Heaven-on-Earth

Kay Sturgis · Larry Sturgis

Deborah Taylor · Thomas Keller

PENGUIN STUDIO

PENGUIN STUDIO
Published by the Penguin Group
Penguin Books USA Inc., 375 Hudson Street,
New York, New York 10014, U.S.A.
Penguin Books Ltd, 27 Wrights Lane, London W8 5TZ, England
Penguin Books Australia Ltd, Ringwood, Victoria, Australia
Penguin Books Canada Ltd, 10 Alcorn Avenue,
Toronto, Ontario, Canada M4V 3B2
Penguin Books (N.Z.) Ltd, 182–190 Wairau Road,
Auckland 10, New Zealand

Penguin Books Ltd, Registered Offices:
Harmondsworth, Middlesex, England

First published in 1997 by Penguin Studio,
an imprint of Penguin Books USA Inc.

1 3 5 7 9 10 8 6 4 2

Copyright © Angel Talk Inc., 1997
All rights reserved

ISBN: 0–670–86740–3
CIP data available

Printed in Hong Kong

Angel painting by Karen M. Haughy
Angel indicator design by Kimio Honda, Aye–Aye Communications
Book cover and interior design by Kathryn Parise
Board design by Kathryn Parise and Jim Sarfati
Package design by Ben Argueta
Icon line art by Liz Grace
Art direction by Marie Timell

Dedicated to
Kelly Elizabeth Willis,
the courageous soul whose gift
changed our lives forever

Our thanks to:

The One-Who-Created-Us-All

The Angelic Kingdom

Wayne Jennings, for the financial support that helped us to create *The Angels Talk*

Sandra Martin, our agent and friend and beloved Earth Angel who delivered us to Penguin

Bob Friedman, for introducing us to Sandra and lovingly guiding us throughout

Michael Fragnito, whose sixth sense for what is inherently beautiful made *The Angels Talk* possible

Marie Timell, our editor and partner, who lovingly nurtured us to completion

Contents

Section Three
How We Met the Angels

Foreword

Dearest Children of Earth,

Once upon a time in a place not far away, an intention flowed forth from the will of the One-Who-Created-Us-All, through the angels and into the waiting hearts of humanity. Thus, The Angels Talk *was born in the spirit, as all things are.*

The purpose of The Angels Talk *is to help bring Heaven-on-Earth into experience. To fulfill this purpose, a bridge must be built, an actual connection between the Human Kingdom and the One-Who-Created-Us-All. The angels can and will assist in the building of this bridge, and as this connection is forged, a realization, a remembrance of the primary Universal Law that we are all One, will begin to develop. In this way, Heaven-on-Earth will become a reality.*

It is with pure devotion that we give this gift to you. The Angels Talk *is a sacred tool of divination to assist you in experiencing our gift of unconditional love. Playing the game is not an end in itself; rather, it is a means to get you where you wish to go. Nor is it the only path to enlightenment, as truly all paths lead directly to the One. However, know that this "path" has been divinely inspired, and is one that will take you to Heaven-on-Earth quickly and safely.*

You will notice that as you learn to play, not only will we talk with you, we will also begin to form an intimate relationship with one another. When you master this connection with us, you will become more sensitive to the loving energy that emanates eternally from and to the One-Who-Created-Us-All. Once the playing of The Angels Talk is mastered and communications with us are well developed, playing the game may no longer be necessary, for then communications with us will be directly experienced. In the meantime, The Angels Talk will guide you to take the steps to personal ascension and to the experience of Heaven-on-Earth.

The rest of the story, how the The Angels Talk game and companion book came to be, is one that is well worth sharing. When the time was right, a special plan was formed by the angels, one which would integrate with humanity's chosen method of learning. This "chosen" method was and is to gain peace and happiness through pain and suffering. As odd as this may seem, this is the will of the Human Kingdom, although it is not a necessity; and since we cannot interfere with your free will, we had to make allowances accordingly.

Additionally, a "human vehicle" was required to bring this tool to Earth. Thus, as this request was sent forth into the ethers, an experienced and wizened soul known to you as Kelly Elizabeth Willis came forward and volunteered for the assignment. Kay, Larry, Deborah, and Thomas, and a host of others also joyfully agreed to help in fulfilling the intention.

In accepting the mission, Kelly agreed to be born with a life-threatening disease. True to what we knew would occur, her mother, Kay, plunged into emotional despair. Yet, out of this suffering, arose an intention to seek the underlying truth of the experience. The process of uncovering this truth took twelve of your Earth years to come about, and during this time, Kelly struggled with her condition. At long last, when *death was close by, the door to Kay's heart finally swung open, and in we stepped with a "vision" of the game. At that time, a miracle flowed forth from the One-Who-Created-Us-All, and a healing occurred, so that Kelly could continue living to fulfill the remainder of her life purpose on Earth. Thus, the gift of* The Angels Talk *came into earthly manifestation, and into your hands.*

In Chapter One, Deborah has laid out the fundamental structure of how anyone can play The Angels Talk. *In Chapter Two, Kay describes a profound journey called "Initiation into Self," which you can choose to embark upon, along with the angels, to realize the promise of Heaven-on-Earth. We will share our story about the relationship between the Human and Angelic Kingdoms in Chapters Three, Four, and Five. Chapter Six contains questions and answers to satisfy and stimulate further curiosity about our world. In Chapters Seven through Ten, you will read about the four co-creators of* The Angels Talk *and the stories of their personal "Initiation into Self." Finally, in Chapter Eleven, Larry describes how the co-creators of* The Angels Talk *came to embrace the "Spirit of Cooperation" and how the original concept of Heaven-on-Earth became a reality for the group.*

It is our faithful prayer that you, too, will choose to take this journey with us, and to this end, you will also join us in celebrating a renewed way of living, one that expresses the desire to live according to the Universal Law that we are One! Through this heartfelt desire, we can, and will, create Heaven-on-Earth together. We are with you, and we love you. We invite you to begin.

—THE ANGELS

Introduction

> The Angels Talk *is a gift that we freely offer*
> *out of the intention of unconditional love for*
> *humanity, for those who would join us in creating*
> *Heaven-on-Earth.*
>
> —THE ANGELS

*S*eptember 1994, a gorgeous Indian summer in Virginia
Beach—the best part of the year. The beaches were empty
and the sky was robin's egg blue. Yet we hardly noticed the
weather, so hard at work were we on designing a game that
might somehow help twelve-year-old Kelly Willis talk to
the angels.

Kelly had been suffering from a serious liver disease and
had been on an organ-transplant list for seven months. She
was growing increasingly weaker and afraid for her future.
She had asked her mother to find a way for her to receive
comfort from the angels. After desperately praying for a
way to assist her, Kay received a vision: a game that Kelly
could use to talk with the angels. Kay asked her husband,
Larry, to help her create the game for Kelly, and he readily

agreed. Not knowing much about angels, they sought the knowledge of their friends Deborah and Thomas, who had written *Angels: The Lifting of the Veil*. And so, this project began. In the beginning, we weren't sure what to call the game, so we asked Kelly, who quickly named it *The Angels Talk,* and so it was and is.

Along the way, the angels played a pivotal role in assisting Kelly in dealing with her fears and, ultimately, receiving a liver transplant that saved her life. We also came to understand that these glorious beings had even greater plans for *The Angels Talk.* They wanted all of humanity to have access to it, and thus, you now have the same opportunity as we: to experience a profoundly intimate relationship with the angels.

None of us will ever forget that first day when the game board was finally complete, and after a fervent prayer, we sat to play. Lo and behold, it worked! With Kay on one side of the board and Larry on the other, their hands gently placed on the plastic angel pointer, it began inching its way across the board, spelling out the first greeting from the angels: *"We are with you, and we love you."* There wasn't a dry eye among us.

As the weeks and months flew by, and we continued to play *The Angels Talk,* we became privy to an entirely new perspective on life and acquainted with the colorful troupe of angels assigned to assist us. Michael spoke to us first, a passionate and rather awesome archangel, whose messages, as spelled out letter-by-letter across the board, were so profound they caused goose bumps to go up and down our spines. We encountered others: the Angelic Scholars, for example, whose wellspring of angelic wisdom on virtually any subject seemed infinite, and whose rousing tongue-in-cheek sense of humor often had us in stitches. For instance, once Larry asked the angels for a "progress report" after taking a rather significant step in his personal life, the Angelic Scholars responded—jokesters that they are—with simply *"By Alfred, you've got it."*

When we consider the transformation that took place in our own lives while learning to play *The Angels Talk,* we are amazed and humbled. During the first few months of playing the game, the angels took some getting used to; yet as we became more comfortable and relaxed with their subtle "energy" moving through our bodies, more sophisticated messages began to emerge. We had to learn about angels much like one would learn about any subject—a step at a time. As fate would have it, just as we were adjusting to these amazing communications, we discovered this companion book was to be written. We set to work immediately, and when we asked the angels if they would give us an outline for the book, they did—effortlessly.

During the game session when the angels gave us the book's outline, they also spelled out that they would like to have a section in our book just for themselves—for their very own story. Here they would tell the heartwarming story of Creation and of the once-intimate and loving relationship between the Human and Angelic Kingdoms that has deteriorated over time. Most important, they would share with us how to recover what humanity has forgotten. We couldn't wait to get started, but the angels said they could not dictate this section until we'd finished our own chapters. In these chapters, they gave us the task of telling our own stories. We weren't sure at first why this was so, but our trust in these glorious beings had grown, and so, without question, we dove into writing.

We began to write "our" chapters and waited for them to write theirs. In the interim, we were thrust into an experience that literally transformed every area of our lives, riveting our attention on our relationship with the angels as well as ourselves, and greatly expanding our capacity to receive angelic messages. They called this the "Initiation into Self," and it seemed to be a map to a place called Heaven-on-Earth. As they accompanied us along its paths—we discovered it was a journey of self-discovery.

Playing *The Angels Talk* can be the beginning of a powerful journey into greater awareness. Not simply greater awareness of the legions of angels at our beck and call but of the deep, inner wisdom we all carry in our hearts. When we began to write this book, we naively thought our greatest challenge was how, in heaven's name, to convey the awesomeness of what can happen when you play *The Angels Talk*. This wasn't the case. Our greatest challenge was, in the face of the nearly constant presence of beings who are so unconditionally loving, so free, and so willing to show us how to dance through life, being brought face-to-face with everything in ourselves that was unlike that pure freedom: the fear, the judgments, the attachments, all of the many ways we turned away from the still, small voice of the heart. But with the angels as celestial role models, we used the game to understand and experience life in a brand-new way—and take it from us, it works. Our lives have changed gradually, but dramatically, and we have begun to experience glimpses of the life we'd always hoped was possible.

So whether you choose to play *The Angels Talk* as a lighthearted game of discovery or as a tool for developing greater consciousness, buckle your seat belts and prepare to embark on a journey that may change your life. *The Angels Talk* changed ours.

Section One

*

How to Play
The Angels Talk

Chapter One

How to Talk
with the Angels

This is a game in which one can directly contact the angels and begin a process that will bring you to a place in life of love, joy, peace, and more. The more you play, the better the link with the angels.
—THE ANGELS

*T*he Angels Talk is a tool to help you learn how to communicate with the angels. It allows the angels to offer their love and support to you, and it fulfills their wish to help you remember that Heaven-on-Earth is possible—and that they are here to help you create it. We recommend that you read this chapter carefully before playing the game. As you read, always keep in mind that learning to communicate with the angels is like learning a new language—the language of the heart.

What Is an Angel?

Believe and expect and you will know us. If you wait until we are seen in the flesh, you will miss the first steps and hamper your timing. We communicate directly to your inner senses. So believe and listen, and do not discount the voices, visions, feelings within—for if you accept and believe, you can also know it is us. We always come. We are not always acknowledged.

—THE ANGELS

The answer to the question "What is an angel?" could fill a book, and even then, we may only hint at who and what they truly are. The word, of course, means "messenger," and while they are indeed the messengers of the One-Who-Created-Us-All, they are so much more: awesome, luminous, holy, and always with us. Yet they must wait for us to invite them into our lives, and when we do, they love us so utterly and deliciously that we are never the same again.

Yet, as wondrous as these celestials beings are, there are certain qualities that take some getting used to. For one thing, angels remain—for the most part—invisible. This is because the energy that makes up their beingness is of a slightly higher vibrational frequency than the one our physical senses are able to discern. Moreover, the language of angels is wordless. They speak in the form of pure thought —telepathically, or "mind to mind"—and we experience these messages as feelings, thoughts, and instincts. In fact, those of us who claim to communicate with angels admit that we often cannot see them or even hear them speak; we "feel" them in the form of hunches or odd, serendipitous coincidences that help us realize that "someone" has our best interests at heart. Or we may suddenly "know" something, even though there is no logical proof to it, and then, lo and behold, it turns out to be true. Because of this, no two encounters with angels are alike, and there is no "right" way to communicate with them. The best advice is to trust one's feelings, since it is through feelings that you'll know when angels are hovering in your midst.

In order to tune in to your feelings and learn to speak with angels, it is important to become more in touch with your senses and their effect on your inner awareness—to, as the angels say, *"hear, smell, taste, see, and feel in a more refined manner."* So, as you play *The Angels Talk,* pay special attention to what you are feeling, what you sense—all the subtle sounds, sights, and sensations—because if you ask to get to know the angels better, rest assured, legions will flock to your assistance in an angelic minute.

Preparing to Dialogue with the Angels

The intention that one holds when approaching the game would hopefully be prayerful; begin each game experience with a sacred intent and attitude.
—The Angels

Spending a few moments in preparation before playing *The Angels Talk* is very important. According to the angels, the first and most important step before playing the game is to "set your intention." The intention you have when you play *The Angels Talk* can make the difference between an experience that can change your life and "just another experience."

To set your intention simply means to make a conscious

decision about why you want to play the game and your hoped-for outcome. In short, your intention is your choice, and once you set it, the angels will help you to bring your choice into reality. You see, angels can't interfere with your free-will choices—that's not their job. They can only assist with what you choose with your own free will. So take a moment to decide why you are playing and what you hope to accomplish. For example, "I intend that this *The Angels Talk* session help me solve my issue with _____." It is always helpful to speak your intention out loud; however, if you wish to keep your intention private, and simply think it to yourself, it is all right. Remember that the angels always hear you.

Attitude is another important consideration. *The Angels Talk* was created with a very special intention in mind: it is a sacred tool for consciousness and a gift of love. That means it's important to have consideration for those whom you invite into your life. Remember that you're inviting celestial beings to speak with you, and they are just as "real" as any other person—whether you can see them or not. Remember also that they come bearing very precious gifts of love, inspiration, and wisdom. So it's a good idea to be considerate and treat them with honor and respect. Also remember that the only beings allowed to speak to you through *The Angels Talk* are angels.

While we're on the subject of attitude, here is another suggestion for effortless communication with the angels. Become childlike. Not child-ish—child-like. Remember when you were a child, how free and trusting you were? This simple trust and belief, that virtually anything is possible, will help banish any doubts that might crop up about communicating with angels. Also remember how, by using your imagination, you could create anything you wanted? It is the imaginative part of yourself that can communicate easily and effortlessly with angels: imagination is the doorway. As the angels have often said, *"Whatever you can conceive, you can achieve."* So, in summary, as you prepare to play: first, set your intention; second, take a moment to note your own attitude and adjust it, if need be, to one of respect and mindfulness; finally, prepare your heart, become like a child, and let your imagination flow freely, trusting and believing that the angels are with you.

Creating an Angelic Atmosphere

The angels suggest that you and—if there are other players—your partners prepare what they call a "sacred space" for playing the game. A sacred space is an environment designated as holy and devoted to meeting with emissaries of the One-Who-Created-Us-All. It should be a quiet place, where you can unplug the phone and forget all your worldly concerns. You may wish to prepare this space by conducting a special ceremony, such as lighting a candle, burning incense or sage, ringing a tiny bell, or saying a blessing. The point is to focus your intention on setting the stage for playing, so you and your partners can relax and the angels can feel at home.

Phrasing Your Questions

Those playing should make a list of the questions they wish to ask the angels before beginning to play *The Angels Talk*. The angels have repeatedly emphasized to us the importance of knowing what we wanted to ask, before we began to play. Confusing questions bring about confusing answers. Sincere questions bring about sincere answers. Silly questions result in silly answers. So, for the clearest answer possible, try to phrase your question in clear, simple terms. For example, you might ask the angels, "What do I need to do to have a closer relationship with you?" Or, "Can you please help me understand how I can find a job that I love?"

It is also important to understand that the angels can only offer information on subjects about which you have knowledge. In other words, if you are asking about Einstein's theory of relativity but have no understanding of physics, it is difficult for the angels to phrase their answer so that it can be understood by the player. They need to, as they say, "get a hook" on the person asking the question—that is, a basis of comprehension so that the answer will be understood.

Try very hard to have a sense of "non-attachment" about your question. In other words, when you ask a question, ask about what you genuinely want to know. Don't ask a question for confirmation of what you have already decided is the answer, or with the hope of receiving the answer you would like to hear. Sometimes it is hard not to have a strong desire for a particular response, but it is best to avoid questions such as these. Remember, *sincerely* seeking wisdom or knowledge on a matter works best with the angels.

How to Play The Angels Talk

The Angels Talk contents:
- *The Angels Talk* companion book
- Playing board
- Angel pointer: The plastic angel-shaped guide that

allows the message from the angels to flow through your hands and move across the board.

What you will need:
- Writing pad
- Pen and/or pencil
- Tape recorder (optional)

The Angels Talk can be played alone or with one or more partners. We found it far easier, more satisfying, and simply more fun when we played together. When we asked the angels why, they said it was because when two or more people come together with the same intention, the intention becomes stronger. It also inspired us to help one another, and when we did, the angels responded with great delight, since the subject of cooperation is one they hold near and dear.

Step One: Setup

To begin, place the board on a small table, on the corner of a large table, or on the floor. A level surface is important, so that the pointer can move freely. Wipe the board with a soft cloth, to remove all dust. If you are playing with partners, sit close enough so that two people can rest their fingers on the pointer, or indicator, comfortably.

Have pen and paper ready; you will need it to keep track of the letters the angels point to. It will also give you a record of what the angels have said to you. In fact, you might wish to keep an "angel notebook" to preserve the records of your meetings with the angels in one place. If you are playing with partners, designate one person to call out the letters, or icons, and another as "angel secretary" to write them down. If you are playing alone, call out your questions and answers into a tape recorder. It's always a good idea to use a tape recorder as backup. Once you learn how to play effortlessly, the angels will spell out words so fast you may lose your concentration, and before you know it, you're quite a few letters behind. If this happens, as it often did with us, simply ask the angels to stop and pick up with the last word you wrote down.

Next, designate who will have the contact with the angel pointer. Remember, the angelic energy moves through your body and onto the board. One or more players at a time can place their fingertips of both hands on the pointer. We consider two people to be ideal, but three works well also. More than three seems to only create confusion, due to the many arms stretched out across the board. Before making contact with the angel pointer, it's a good idea for those selected to rub their hands together briskly. This allows the angelic energy to more easily move through the body. Those in contact with the angel pointer should make sure that their fingers stay firmly, but very gently, in contact with it. This will allow it to slide easily across the board. Too much pressure can stop it from moving. Certainly the pointer should not be pushed or pulled. Remember, the angels are in charge.

Before beginning to play, you may want to experiment with the indicator by moving it around the board to get a feel for the flow of its movement. Next, decide who will go first and take turns moving in a clockwise direction around the board. We recommend that the youngest player go first, but the choice is up to you and/or your partner(s). Now that the players' roles and turns have been determined, pen and paper are in hand, and the tape recorder is turned on, place the angel pointer at the center of the board. You are ready to begin talking with angels.

Step Two: Invite the Angels to Play

When you are ready, close your eyes and, if you are playing with partners, hold hands and call in your angelic friends. Use your imagination and visualize yourself surrounded by angels. Take a few deep breaths, breathing in their love. Then ask for their assistance by saying aloud, or to yourself, "I call on the angels from the Throne of Grace to be with me as I play." This is a very important step. Remember, angels don't have permission from the One-Who-Created-Us-All to just barge into our lives; they are polite, and they wait for our invitation.

Step Three: The Angels Talk

You are now ready to speak directly to your celestial friends. The first player asks his or her question aloud. When you have asked your question, wait quietly until the pointer begins to move. Initially the pointer may move slowly and/or begin to circle the board and hover near certain symbols or letters before stopping. You may want to begin with simple "yes" or "no" questions so you can get used to the feeling of the angels moving the pointer under your fingertips. Remember that the players in contact with the board must keep at least three or four fingertips of both hands on the angel pointer at all times while playing. Players should wait until they are certain that the message is complete before removing their hands. Failure to keep contact may cause the angel pointer to stop moving. When the angels have completed their message and are ready for the next question, the angel pointer will return to the center of the board.

Receiving Your Answer

The angels may respond to your questions in a number of ways. They may cause the pointer to move toward one of the twenty-six letters of the alphabet to spell out your answer, or to indicate either a "yes" or "no" response, or to point to one of the icons. When the answer is to be spelled out, the intended letter will appear in the center of the angel pointer. This letter should be called out and written down before the pointer moves on to the next letter. When the message indicator stops moving or returns to the center of the board, the message is complete. The angels are finished with their answer.

You may wish to read the message aloud after each question, or you can wait until everyone has received an answer. (If you're like us, you probably won't want to wait any longer than necessary!) Whatever the answer, make sure you record it. Often when you look back over your notes, you will discover new meaning in your answers. If you find your answer to be unclear, simply ask the angels for clarification or to restate the answer.

It is important to remember that there is no reason to be afraid of the answers the angels will give you. Their answers are always, always, always loving, kind, nonjudgmental, and frequently very funny! They do not reveal anything about you unless you wish it to be revealed. This loving attitude should be your cue when you are playing in a group. When reading answers out loud, do not try to interpret someone else's answer unless he or she asks you to do so—even if you believe that you are only trying to be helpful. The angels know exactly how to speak to each one of us, and their answers are perfectly formed for the one asking the question. Only that person can understand the answer, even if full comprehension occurs at a later time. (This was often the case with us.)

Do Angels Make Mistakes?

What happens when the message you receive is incorrect? While this didn't happen to us often, when it did, we'd mope around for days, secretly harboring concerns that perhaps the whole idea of the game was a bust! When we finally got the courage to consult the angels as to why this happened, they gave us a mini-lesson in non-attachment. *"When you are attached emotionally to a response, you will find the answer distorted to the degree of your attachment. Emotional resistance is an energy that causes distortion—particularly with issues having to do with 'having.'"* In other words, when you ask the angels about something that matters a great deal to you, your degree of attachment to a particular outcome or point of view can scramble the reception. Why? Simply because of your willfulness, you may be a little reluctant to hear the truth.

You may also notice that, at times, the angels' spelling leaves something to be desired. The angels tell us that misspelled words occur when energy in the players' physical bodies are blocked, or when players are not so hot at spelling themselves. You see, messages, even from the angelic realm, are colored by the one who receives them—

colored by our beliefs and also, unfortunately, by our vocabulary. As they ever so gently suggested, *"When your programming suggests misspelling, it's easier to transmit what is already there in your mind than to assist in reprogramming. Anyway,"* they said, with their typical hilarity, *"nowhere in the universe is it a sin to misspell words, except in the wee minds of those whose only recognized gift is the ability to spell with a flourish. And they, too, will have the choice to become One."* So, if the spelling of the messages is bad, bad, bad—not to worry. The angels will give you an *A* regardless.

When the Answer Is an Icon

If the pointer moves to one of the eight icons, record it and then use your intuition to interpret the meaning as it pertains to your question. Usually when the angels point to an icon, they are suggesting a way for you to find additional answers to your question. According to the angels, each icon is the method best suited for you, to tap into your potential here on earth.

Art, whether in the form of writing, reading, painting, drawing, sculpting, dancing, or acting, is a tool to align you to what the angels call the "creative wellspring" of your soul. **Music** can alter your state of mind and bring you to new and higher levels of consciousness. By attuning you to a higher level of energy, it is also an excellent way to sense the presence of angels in your midst. Keeping a **journal** and **meditating** can help you become more familiar with your own inner wisdom, as well as that of the angels. **Nature,** according to the angels, is where any answer to any possible question about life is available to you. By immersing yourself in the natural world—taking a walk in the woods or a park, spending time in your garden, hiking or boating—you will find that the answer or insight you are looking for will come to mind. If the pointer indicates **The Body,** it means the angels are recommending that you embark on a new program of bodywork or exercise. Whether it is yoga, dance, sports, or "working out," they are encouraging you to become more aware and in touch with your physical self. **Dreams** means the angels are suggesting that you will acquire the information you need by paying attention to your dreams and spending some time deciding what they are telling you. You may wish to begin a dream journal in which you write down your dreams when you wake up each morning. Study this journal and reflect on what the symbols in the dreams mean to you. Finally, if the pointer moves to the icon termed **Attribute,** this means that the angels wish to spell out an attribute for you that will allow you to know and experience your soul's purpose. An attribute is a characteristic or quality, one that can be developed and reinforced within oneself, that will help you fulfill your soul's mission. The angels would never just tell you your attribute, you must request it of them. (For more information on attributes, see Chapter Two.) If you have already received an attribute during a previous session, this is a message to focus on it more consistently to discover the answer to your present question.

When There Is No Answer

When that pivotal moment arrives and you and your playing partner(s) first put your hands on the pointer and ask a question, what happens when nothing happens? First of all, relax. Communication can break down for any number of reasons. Low physical energy on the part of the players can be one reason. One way to get the indicator to move is to give it a nudge. Often this is all it takes to send it sailing across the board. Or you may need to go back over the steps outlined in this chapter and check your intention and attitude. Some adjustment to these may be called for. If there is no answer or the angel pointer appears to act "crazy," or go off the edge of the board, be patient. As the angels say, *"When there is difficulty, or when the pointer doesn't seem to move, or what is spelled out makes no sense, it is simply the illusion of doubt and fear. Have faith."* It may take some time, but eventually everyone can learn to talk to the angels.

Practice will improve your skills and open the channels of communication between you and the angels. We, too, were shaky in the beginning. Sometimes the pointer wouldn't budge, or when it did, it spelled out gobbledy-gook. Yet each time we played, it got easier. (With a team of Angelic Scholars cheering us on, how could we lose!) Even when we thought we were progressing very slowly, they simply chalked it up to a learning curve. *"You cannot necessarily expect instant gratification. Learning to play is rather like fine wine. It is a process."* So be patient and trust that the angels want to communicate with you as much as you want to communicate with them.

Signs That May Accompany Angelic Communications

You may notice that after you or your partner(s) ask a question, you begin to "hear" the message in your mind before it is spelled out. This is a bit disarming in the beginning since, when the pointer spells out what you just heard, if you're like us, you may begin to wonder who's communicating with whom. When we asked the angels why this occurred, they were obviously amused and applauded us, saying they were just priming the pump. *"What you are actually 'getting' is necessary and will help you receive direct communications from us in the future. So continue to practice until you have graduated. After the pump is primed, the fresh, clean water begins to flow—and so it is with our messages!"* Eventually we began calling out the messages we received before the angels had finished spelling, and if we were correct in our intuition, the pointer would return to the starting point or the "yes" position—presumably to indicate that "we'd got it, by Alfred."

You may also notice a number of odd sensations as you play. You might, for instance, experience goose bumps or tingling at the back of your neck. Or you may experience a feeling of indescribable sweetness, as if you are suddenly flooded with love and tenderness. Often when this happens, it's difficult to hold back the tears. Let them flow. This is simply the opening of the heart that naturally occurs in the presence of such unconditionally loving beings. You may also catch an intoxicating whiff of fresh flowers. This is just an indication that the angels are communicating with you "nose to nose." You may also notice your arms and fingers tingling or feel a mild shock when you touch the pointer. This is, according to the angels, simply because they communicate first through our bodies and then through the board. Your back, neck, and arms may also get tired and achy. According to the angels, this can happen when you are unaccustomed to the flow of angelic energy. As you continue to play *The Angels Talk,* you will begin to know when to stop because the high-voltage energy of the angels has tired you or it is time for a short break to stretch.

Happy Trails, Partners

Congratulations! You've just communicated with the angels. As you become more comfortable with playing, it only gets better. In fact, the more you dialogue with the angels, the more they will share. When you are finished playing, remember to thank them for their assistance.

And now that you've opened the door to communication with the angels, don't turn off your newly developed senses when you put the board away. Remember that the ultimate aim of the angels in co-creating *The Angels Talk* is to teach humans how to communicate with them all the time. Playing *The Angels Talk* is just a first step. Once you've invited your angelic cronies into your life, they will be with you always. So enlist their help as you go about your daily life. Take 'em shopping. Ask them to help you find a parking place. Heck. Take them dancing. They love to have fun. And if you are ready and if it is your wish, the angels have another adventure up their sleeves for you—a profound, transformative journey that they have named "Initiation into Self," especially designed to help you get to know yourself better. Read all about it in Chapter Two.

Chapter Two

Initiation into Self

This chapter presents an "Initiation into Self," where communications with us can be magnified and enhanced; for you to know thyself is truly the ultimate task for humanity at this time. "To remember thyself " is perhaps a better statement.
—THE ANGELS

Choosing to Play The Angels Talk as an "Initiation into Self"

*T*he Angels Talk can certainly be a game, a game of divination, if you will, whereby you discover the answers to questions about your everyday life—work, relationships, health, children. However, if you are seeking more profound answers to spiritual questions, playing *The Angels Talk* on a regular basis can provide them. In other words, you can also play *The Angels Talk* to expand your consciousness, deepen your understanding of yourself and others, and discover greater meaning in the universe.

The angels call this way of playing an "Initiation into Self." It is simply choosing to embark on a journey of self-discovery and transformation, to "remember yourself"—that is, to discover on a profound level, who you are. By playing regularly with this purpose in mind, your ability to communicate directly with the angels improves all the time. This, in turn, enables them to help you and improves your ability to help yourself to achieve greater self-understanding. It's that simple.

This chapter is the "map" of the territory we explored in our journey as we worked with the angels to create *The Angels Talk*. It is our prayer that you, too, will choose to take this transformative journey, by learning to communicate in great depth with the angels, to transform your life on *all* levels. The angels are always willing to answer your questions, and if you are willing, the angels will give you "homework assignments" in the form of suggestions that will guide you on your journey.

Throughout our experience, the angels *always* asked if we were in agreement, letting us know we truly had a choice whether or not to follow their directives. Of course, we always agreed, driven by our desire to connect ever more closely with these beautiful energies and, in the process, remember ourselves. Still, it was comforting to know that, had we chosen not to, they would still love us, assist us, and be with us. There were no conditions placed upon us at any time.

The assignments usually took the form of a specific focus, or even a provocative question. For example, we were asked early on in our quest to *"become receptive to the waves of intention flowing from the Angelic Kingdom through our bodies."* Simply by focusing our minds on the assignment, we did indeed become more receptive to what the angels wished. As you develop your own personal connection with the angels, you will come to understand the "homework assignments," how to fulfill them, and how they were designed specifically for your personal transformation.

Playing Alone or with Others

Before you begin your "Initiation into Self," it is important to consider whether you will be experiencing it alone or with others. If you are going it alone, you can move along the path of initiation at your own pace. If you wish to undergo your "Initiation into Self" with the company and support of others, you may wish to create a more structured approach by getting together with friends, or anyone you trust, once a week or more to play the game, and share what you are learning with each other. Giving and receiving support can inspire you to persevere when the journey seems shadowy or you find yourself in confusing waters. However you choose to play *The Angels Talk,* if your choice is to play it as an "Initiation into Self," then your next step will be to set yourself the goal of purifying your emotional body, thus embarking upon an adventure into remembering who you really are.

Purification of the Emotional Body

We communicate through subtle waves of energy emanating from and to the will of the One-Who-Creates-All-Life. Learn our language so that you may proceed on this mission. **In accepting this**

*assignment, what is of primary impor-
tance is to set your attention on purifying
the emotional body. Consider that incoming
data moves through the perceptual patterning of
this body—as set up through the intention of the
individual will—and that conscious decisions rise
to the surface through this filtering process.*

*When the attention is directed as given above,
you will naturally begin to balance and heal that
which needs these, so that the One-Connecting-All
may be fully realized. During this process, any
truth that has been held separate in the mind
begins to freely express itself as part of the whole
to which it belongs. These previously unaccepted
truths can be called* **shadows.** *Once they are expressed out of the freedom you have given them
through your conscious acknowledgment and the
acceptance That-We-Are-All-One, there is a release of these shadows, so that they, too, as entities,
may move into the light.*

—THE ANGELS

Angels and humans communicate in different languages.
So in order to truly create rapport with each other on
deeper levels, we must learn to speak the same language.
When the angels give us messages as we play *The Angels
Talk,* they are meeting us halfway. As they work, through
the use of our rather limiting words, to assist us in understanding their kingdom, we gain the ability, and perhaps realize a responsibility, to grasp their own enchantingly subtle
forms of expression.

As discussed in Chapter One, the angels communicate

with us through our thoughts, feelings, and instincts—through the "emotional body." Ridding ourselves of any negative thoughts, attitudes, or patterns, purifies this body so that we can receive the angels' form of communication more clearly. It removes the static from the lines.

So, following the angels' instructions, we set out to "purify our emotional bodies." This was truly an educational experience. Rather than study our subject in an objective manner by reading books or interviewing people "in the know," for example, we just followed the angelic directive: to focus our will—set our intention—on the *thought* of purifying our emotional bodies. It was so simple! All we had to do was *choose* this consciously, and we proceeded to learn a great deal.

Vast amounts of literature is available about the nature of our emotions. It's an immense subject, to be sure. Just as our cells are encased in a physical body, our emotions are contained by an "emotional body," which is also like an energy field. Just as our physical body is made up of bones, muscles, nerves, and so on, our emotional body is made up of different parts too: the gamut of our emotional experiences and responses, including all the joy, love, happiness, gratitude, shame, guilt, fear, anger, and a full spectrum of other emotions. Clearly it is far more subtle and sensitive than the physical body, but anyone who has ever felt a single feeling knows that the emotional body does indeed exist.

The angels explain that, as incoming data moves through our emotional body, it is filtered by our perceptual patterning. To simplify this message: first we receive information through our five senses, seeing, hearing, touching, tasting, and smelling; then we process this information through our perceptual filters or our personal cauldron of awareness, which is seasoned with our attitudes, values, and our personal belief systems—our perspective on who we think we are and what life is about. These filters form an intricate web through which the information is colored before it is revealed to the conscious mind.

Unfortunately our perceptual filters become contaminated with dense patterns of energy. These patterns are most often the result of past experiences. The angels say that these impurities are called "shadows" and are parts of ourselves we have yet to become aware of. When these shadows are exposed or brought to our conscious awareness, we have a choice. We can willingly choose to acknowledge them and lovingly send them into the light of truth, or we can give them power over our true nature so that we continue on a path of ignorance and suffering. Most of us persist in our accustomed ways, permitting our shadows to rule us, and eventually these shadows cause us to end our lives here on Earth in pain and suffering. The beauty of knowing all of this is that it doesn't have to be this way. The angels have made this clear. We can change, and when we do, joy becomes a way of life, even through the process of aging and dying.

To demonstrate this concept, consider the following story. There once was a man with a heart condition who was terribly afraid of snakes. Unfortunately the man was called away on a business trip to a foreign country, which was known for its abundant wildlife, including snakes. With some trepidation, and vowing to be constantly aware of anything that moved, he settled into a native bungalow. Later that evening, he returned to his cottage and, upon opening the door, saw before him, in the dark shadows of his room, a long snake stretched out on the floor. He was so filled with fear he died instantly of a heart attack. The next morning, when the housekeeper came to inspect the room, she found him lying next to a length of rope that had fallen from a piece of artwork hanging on the wall. His "snake" was only a simple rope!

When our perceptual filters distort incoming messages, our life experiences simply reflect the distortion. In the preceding story, the man saw a rope; however, his perceptual filter, which was blocked by some past shadowy experience, saw a snake. Further, the coroner, who later signed the death certificate, saw the man's death as a simple heart attack. Since we have a bird's-eye view of the story, it is plain to see that a distorted emotional perception is what really killed the poor guy. How many "snakes" do we see in our lives that are truly nothing but pieces of rope?

To get back to our own story, it was obvious to us that the purification of our emotional bodies, by bringing our shadow qualities into the light, would be absolutely necessary if we were to deepen our relationship with the angels and heal ourselves in the process. But how were we to bring those shadows of past experience into the now and into the light so that they might be accepted, loved, embraced, and integrated, leaving us with purified emotional bodies?

What Is an "Attribute"?

*Intention is a direction or activity of the will. The Angelic Kingdom stands ready to carry out the will of the One-Who-Created-Us-All by aligning with the gift of free will that all human beings have been given, and also by guiding the **purest of humanity's willful intentions or attributes** into manifestation.*

—THE ANGELS

If you wish to deepen your relationship with the Angelic Kingdom, purification of your emotional body, as discussed, is the most important first step. To do this, you must have an "intention" that will lead to this end. Of course, this is true of any worthwhile journey. It is easier if you have a destination in mind. You see, your willful "intention" might be thought of as the vehicle you will use on your journey as you travel toward Heaven-on-Earth. Intention is simply the focusing of your mind. Throughout our work with *The Angels Talk,* the angels told us to "focus, focus, focus." The angels can assist in choosing your intentions, to help you know where you should be placing your focus.

One very important way they assist is to offer you a potent one-word-powerhouse-of-intention called an "attribute." An attribute is simply one of the infinite characteristics or qualities of the One-Who-Created-Us-All. When we chose to ask for and were given an attribute, we were being asked to become conscious and to accept our soul's mission on earth—to actually recognize that we are part of the One, in the here and now. It is our experience that an attribute is that which best meets one's greatest need in the inward expedition. By intending or focusing on your attribute, it purifies your emotional body by showing you the very essence of your soul. Once you glimpse this essence, all your shadows are exposed and all the negative patterning that you have been holding on to seem meaningless and are easily let go of.

The angels are *also* attributes, or qualities, of the One. This means that when they give us an attribute, they are actually giving us the greatest gift of all—the gift of themselves. When you receive your special attribute, the angels will want you to actually *become one of the special angels who personifies that specific attribute!* What an exciting way to learn to communicate with the angels—by actually joining them at their level of being! When you do, an alchemical reaction takes place that brings your shadows into the light, and in the process, purifies your emotional bodies. You can then begin to radiate your attribute into every waking moment of your life—to actually become an "Earth Angel," and express your special attribute in the form of a message from the One-Who-Created-Us-All into the world.

Receiving Your Attribute

Even though this is apparent to us now, when we first "received" our personal attribute, we responded with a simple acknowledgment. The deeper and more profound implications of the assignment took longer to sink in. But as the purification of our perceptual filters occurred, we became so convinced of the power of the assignment, we were able to intensify our focus on it with greater ease. You can read more about our experiences with our attributes in Chapters Eight through Twelve. But right now, you are probably brimming with anticipation over what your own attribute might be. So let's get started and explore some possibilities.

Initially it will be helpful to spend a few minutes perusing the following list of attributes. Take a deep breath and focus on each one. Notice how you feel. This list is in no way complete. After all, how can we possibly list all the qualities of the One-Who-Created-Us-All? However, pondering it will provide the internal "hook" (described in Chapter One) for the angels to "grab" on to when they assign the personal attribute for your journey. In other words, the angels will respond when you resonate with one or another of the attributes.

Transformation	Strength	Freedom
Potential	Balance	Humor
Creativity	Joy	Faith
Gratitude	Focus	Intention
Knowledge	Power	Laughter
Purity	Inspiration	Purpose
Obedience	Deliverance	Spontaneity
Compassion	Order	Surrender
Self-worth	Integrity	Passion
Willingness	Attention	Expectancy
Commitment	Atonement	Expression
Courage	Sisterhood	Flexibility
Emergence	Fulfillment	Inner Authority
Cooperation	Beauty	Communication
Friendship	Release	Nourishment
Listening	Grace	Sustenance
Trust	Tenderness	Wholeness
Delight	Brotherhood	Clarity
Honesty	Harmony	Encouragement
Healing	Good	Blessing
Efficiency	Acknowledgment	Relaxation
Love	Peace	Forgiveness
Prayer	Service	Birth
Abundance	Acceptance	Glory
Adventure	Openness	Truth
Simplicity	Patience	Enthusiasm
Purification	Education	

How did you feel as you turned your attention to each one? Which ones did you feel yourself resonate with? Did you find yourself resisting any of them? Here's what the angels have to say about the list:

Each of the attributes we spelled out are intrinsically re-
lated. All are one, and none are separate from the others.
You can notice how these attributes blend perfectly with
each other and are also interdependently connected. All
roads lead to Rome—or heaven, whatever the case may
be. To avoid the recognition of this truth within yourself
is to sponsor lack in your life. This lack or doubt is what
will be healed during your "Initiation into Self," and
when this happens, we will rejoice! We have come to you
through this means to assist you in remembering what
has been forgotten. As you hear these messages from our
kingdom and hear your individual gift called out, know
that you are the harbinger of that special attribute, and
that you personally are charged with bringing your own
specific attribute into application for all humanity.
What we say to one, we say to all. You cannot possibly
view these attributes for one, and not for all!

—THE ANGELS

How do you receive your attribute? It's simple. Play
The Angels Talk and just ask the angels, "What is my attribute?" Your attribute may or may not come to your mind
before the angels spell it out for you; however, allow them
to go ahead with this. (You'll have plenty of time later to
wonder, as we sometimes did, if perhaps they'd made a mis-
take!) They will then want to know if you will invite and
accept the angels who embody the attribute into your life.
If you agree, you simply state, "I call the Angels of (*your attribute*) to be with me." By asking for their assistance, you
will not have to do all the work by yourself. In fact, the
angels will work with you even when you've forgotten your
"Initiation into Self" and are completely involved with other

things. Read their message at the beginning of the following section and see for yourself the role the angels will play.

Applying Your Attribute

We will be with you consistently from this point always. When you begin and continue to journey with these gifts that are given to you as individuals, so will others do the same. You can then know through the application of this dream that you indeed help each other up the ladder; and you will see, believe, and perceive with all your bodies, hearts, minds, and souls that **all** *of you are indeed One, and that there is no separation between life and itself.*

You will do well to embrace this attribute into your experience and notice how it transforms not only your perceptual patterns, but your whole perspective on life for that matter. We will say to you to pay very intimate attention to all of the aspects and nuances of these given attributes. Learn and integrate these fully, fully, fully. We repeat for emphasis. We say to you, Do this as given and integrate your intended attribute into your physical reality—into your body, heart, mind, and spirit. Apply your attribute into your concept of time— that is, your daily life experiences."

—THE ANGELS

Receiving your attribute is but one part of your "Initiation into Self." Applying and integrating your attribute into your daily experience will bring it to life. To do so, begin focusing on it whenever possible, knowing that when you do, your "perceptual filters" will begin to purify and your communications with the angels will become more refined. As the angels say, *"Wherever you place your focus, expansion will occur."* So call on the angels of your attribute often—to remind yourself of their presence. Let them know you are open to their continued assistance in your life. Contemplate the purpose of this gift. Look the attribute, the word itself, up in the dictionary. Discover it's obvious, as well as deeper, meanings—just as when you learn any new word—and then notice how it mysteriously pops up in discussions more frequently. In fact, you may begin to hear your attribute mentioned time and time again, for example on television, in books, and in casual conversation. Pay attention, for these are signs and messages from the angels. Also pay attention to the thoughts that are in your mind as you "stumble" across your attribute, for this will stimulate further self-development.

You may also want to write your attributes on cards and place them around your home and office in conspicuous places, such as over the telephone, in the kitchen, bathroom, or next to the bed. This will serve as a gentle reminder of your intention. Also notice your thoughts before you speak, asking yourself, "How is (*your attribute*) speaking through me? What would I say in this situation if I were the angel of (*your attribute*)? What action would I take if I were the angel of (*your attribute*)?"

At this point, you may also want to ask the angels for a "progress report" each time you play the game. In this way, you will be supported by the angels in the "Initiation into Self" and the journey to embrace your attribute. The angels will gently guide you back to your intention when you have gone off track. When the four of us would ask for our weekly "reports," the angels would acknowledge our progress and add just enough "food for thought" about what might be done to take another step. Frequently our reports would cause yet another breakthrough in our understanding. This deepening of our awareness would enable our communications with them, as well as with ourselves and each other, to unfold more gracefully than ever before. Sometimes the angelic messages would be so incredibly uplifting, we would find ourselves inexplicably bursting into tears. It felt as if our emotional bodies were indeed transforming right before our very eyes.

Keeping a Journal

Our messages first enter your awareness, taking root within. When you go back and read what has been shared, the perceptual filters have already begun to alter, and naturally, the understanding is greater. As you will experience, this understanding then continues to grow.

—THE ANGELS

Keeping a journal of your journey into remembering the self and recording each one of the angelic messages you receive is strongly recommended. It is also a great way to further integrate your attribute into your own experience and to acknowledge and bring your shadow qualities into the light, thereby helping to purify the emotional body. Include in the journal, one that may be especially earmarked for your journey, the angelic messages you receive and your responses, your "progress reports," and all the experiences and dreams you have during your "Initiation into Self." When you periodically review your journal, you will most likely experience sudden, and previously unexplored, insights—ones you might have missed if you hadn't been able to take a second look at them.

Occasionally, while playing *The Angels Talk,* it seemed as though we had momentarily entered into a trance, since what had occurred during the play was a bit of a blur to us later. When we went back to read over the messages, we were sometimes surprised. We would wonder, were we actually present and conscious while playing the game? If so, why didn't we realize then what was actually said? Why were we so confused when, in retrospect, it all made perfect sense? The angels say it's because their messages can be understood on many different levels, and each time we take a step in our inner growth, we comprehend the message in a new way. By keeping a record of our sessions, we were able to get the most out of the messages. Hopefully, this will be true for you, too.

Another reason for keeping a journal is, according to the angels, when you record your experiences, you are actually *applying* the information from inside yourself through the physical body—your arms, hands, and fingers—and into the world via a pen or keyboard. Thus, the act of writing in a journal tends to "ground" the knowledge into your present experience, making it easier to understand. This is especially important given that we are playing with ethereal creatures like our friends the angels.

In addition, the angels gave us the following questions to contemplate and respond to in our journals. According to the angels, writing out the answers will help you to purify the emotional body and remember more fully your true Self. Choose a few or all of them and journal the answers.

Questions from the Angels

What does spirituality mean to you?

What do you most need or want?

What would you like to change about the way you communicate with other people?

What would you like to change about yourself?

What makes you feel safe and secure?

Do you feel comfortable giving to others? If not, why not?

Do you feel comfortable receiving from others? If not, why not?

What does your body need most?

What needs to be healed in your life?

What is important to you?

What do you like about yourself?

What is one way you can love yourself?

What would bring you joy?

What is a good reason for living on planet Earth?

What secret about yourself would you like to bring out into the open?

Do you ever feel angry with the One? Why?

Can you see, hear, or feel the presence of your Guardian Angels? If so, when and how?

If an angel suddenly appeared and said, "Ask me anything you like," what would you ask?

What could happen to make you more prosperous?

How do you feel about your body?

Define self-worth?

How do you feel about the angels and why?

What is your most important dream?

What does "play" mean to you, and what kind of play do
    you like best?

Do you feel comfortable when you are alone? Why or
    why not?

What can you personally do today to make the world a
    better place in which to live?

What would you like to change about your past?

What would you really like to know about heaven?

What would make you happy?

Whenever the angel pointer moves to the icon "Journaling," it means that the angels would like you to do journal
work in order for you to further your "Initiation into Self."

Meditation

Meditation is the act of silently contemplating a sacred
intention. It is another beneficial tool that will help you
become more familiar with your attribute and yourself.
When we sit and quiet ourselves in meditation, we are able
to listen to the deeper voices inside us—the ones often ignored in our busy lives. Some of these "voices" include
those of the angels, who can communicate more easily with
us while our minds are quiet. As a consequence, we become
more sensitive to inner guidance and allow our attribute to
"speak" to us from within, directing us toward the goal of
purifying our emotional bodies. At one point along the way
on our own journey, we thought it might be useful to ask
the angels for a guided meditation that would assist us with
the integration of our attributes. As always, they responded
instantly, spelling out the following instruction:

Find a quiet place to contemplate your attribute. Allow yourself to slow down, stilling your body, your emotions, and your thoughts—setting your daily concerns aside for a few moments. You can have them back, if you like, when you are done. Move your attention now to your breathing, and observe your inhalations and exhalations while concentrating on slowing them down and breathing more deeply at the same time. Move your focus to the area of your body where your heart is and pretend to breathe directly into your heart. When this becomes natural, begin to silently speak the word representing your attribute. Sense it moving in and out of your heart with each of your breaths. You may take this meditation another step by bringing a problem or something you would like to work with into focus. Bring the idea of it into your heart, and then speak your attribute, breathing it into the matter, breath by breath. On the inhale, your problem, or focus, will be washed and cleansed with the "energy" of your attribute. On the exhale, your patterns, which created the issue, will be resolved and healed. When you feel complete, you may resume your normal activities. Most likely you will shortly experience a deeper clarity and healing of your old problem in your everyday life, and will also notice a shift in your perceptual awareness.

—THE ANGELS

When we practiced this meditation, we were amazed at the power of it. In the beginning, we could only hold our focus for a few moments. Yet after daily practice, we found that virtually any issue we were presently dealing with subconsciously would rise to the surface of our conscious awareness, and a solution would often present itself or the problem would be resolved. As we continued to bring our attribute into sharper focus, we found ourselves living this meditation in each and every moment, fully and completely, as though it were another part of our being. We hope that you may also find yourself awed and amazed at the beauty of this healing and transcendent meditation. Meditation is especially important if the angel pointer moves to the icon when you are playing the game. This means that the angels wish for you to practice meditation as a means to further understand Self.

Dreams

It is often easier for us to work with you while you are sleeping and/or dreaming, because at those times, you are more open to our subtle suggestions.
—THE ANGELS

If you wish it, the angels will come to you through your dreams, offering comfort, healing, encouragement, or even assistance with a problem. As the angels tell us above, dreaming can be another way to communicate with them. Whether you readily recall your dreams or not, it is possible to develop the ability to "hear" the angels' messages through your dreams.

There are several methods that will enhance your success at developing this profound tool through which the angels will often assist you. You might simply begin by writing yourself a note to encourage dreams of your attribute and angels, and then tuck it under your pillow before falling asleep. Another approach might be to state, "I will dream of angels tonight," and then repeat it throughout the day at one and a half hour intervals. This time frame corresponds with the sleep cycles we move through each night. You may also want to use the following affirmation as you are falling off to sleep: "I relax, fall asleep, and dream of (*your attribute*)." (If you wish to encourage your recall, you might want to add "And I will remember my dreams" to the other phrases.) When your dream appears after making these requests, simply trust that the dream will hold an angelic message for you, whether or not an angel actually came into view. Sometimes they appear directly; at other times, they will appear as a wise teacher, guide, animal, or even in the form of a special message.

All four of us used these methods, and each of us had many dreams of angels while co-creating this project. One of us dreamed of thousands of radiantly beautiful angels flying around her throughout the night. Another time, tiny little Dresden-like angels fluttered about her neck and head, speaking to her and telling her stories of the Angelic Kingdom—and healing her headache.

In one of Larry's dreams, he saw his Guardian Angel standing by his side, pointing to a picture of a map on a nearby wall. The "map" had a black background with thick white lines in the shape of a fan. At the bottom center of the fan, where the white lines met, was another thicker white line, like a stem, extended downward. As Larry and the angel moved closer to the picture, they stepped in and onto the map, which instantly became larger than life. Together they stood at the point where all the paths converged, facing the white lines that had now become roads or paths reaching out before them as far as they could see. A single path extended behind them into infinity. The angel pointed in front of them to the path at the extreme left and spoke the name "Michael," and the name automatically spelled itself out upon the path. The angel continued speaking the names of many other angels, and as he did so, the names would appear on their own special paths. In the morning, he awoke with the names of angels ringing in his head. It will be particularly important for you to pay attention to your dreams whenever the icon "Dreams" is indicated while you are playing the game. Expect a very important message or insight from the angels!

Nature

*The study of nature will reveal to you the secrets of the universe. **All the answers** to all your questions about life are perfectly reflected in the natural world.*

—THE ANGELS

As you can see above, the angels have told us that observing and respecting nature is very important. Nature contains "*all the answers to all our questions!*" What a powerful statement! So, what is this concept saying about nature and why is it a great teacher? It really is quite simple, even though the natural world—the universe—is beyond complexity. Within the natural world, all of the attributes of the One-Who-Sustains-All-Life—beauty, truth, purity, simplicity, fulfillment, grace, determination, etc.—are present. This natural world, if we choose to see it, will reflect back to us the perfect unfolding of a beautiful tapestry designed by the One-Who-Creates-Us-All. Throughout evolution, the natural world has remained constant in its fulfillment of itself and the ability to sustain physical life. Although its pristine beauty and purity can be temporarily altered by our will to dominate and change it, left alone, its quality of eternally adhering to the will of the One-Who-Created-Us-All causes it to always emerge victorious. If we can take nature as an example and learn to always allow the will of the One to work through us, we too will emerge as a victor. We can then become part of the harmony of the Cosmos.

There are many paths we can take to begin harmonizing with the natural world. When we take time out of our complicated lives to walk by the seashore, hike through the woods, feed the birds, play with our pets, study rocks, crystals, and plants, and explore other natural wonders, we find ourselves emotionally recharged and refreshed—and we are rejuvenated with this profound connection to life and ourselves.

To begin connecting with the natural world, look around your home and observe what is natural. Do you have clothes made of natural fibers? These fibers have a story to tell. Do you have houseplants? Pets? You can learn from these by closely observing their natural characteristics. Do you have a yard or a garden? Can you take time to be outdoors for an hour, a day, a month? Be sure to spend time in nature on a regular basis, especially if you have received a message from the angels to do so. They will let you know that this is necessary for your "Initiation into Self" by pointing to the "Nature" icon as you play the game. If you set your intention to learn from nature, great riches await you, and according to the angels, all your questions shall be answered.

Art

All, all, all humans are endowed with creative abilities. One of the most positive means of becoming attuned with one's creative wellspring is through artistic endeavors.

—THE ANGELS

How many times have you heard the following statement: "Oh, but I'm not creative. I used to paint, write, dance, play the guitar, etc., when I was a child, but not anymore. Besides, everyone knows that artists starve. I have to be practical." Then with a shrug of the shoulders, the subject is changed. In addition, our schools label classes in art, music, or woodworking as "electives." In other words, you can choose them, but it's not necessary or, for that matter, even important.

The angels give us a different message. They say artistic creativity is one of the most positive means of getting in touch with the deeper parts of ourselves. Indeed, creating something nurtures and encourages not only the expression of our attribute, but also the part of ourselves that is innocent and childlike—that part that communicates most easily with the angels. A creative cycle begins when we foster our creative abilities. Creative expression enhances our sense of a greater Self and, thereby, our connection to the One-Who-Created-Us-All. As this occurs, our emotional body responds and our creative ability expands, and the glorious cycle repeats itself. Don't forget that our creativity is the most direct expression of the creative will of the One.

The task, then, is to get creative! When the angel pointer

moves to the "Art" icon as you play the game, it means that creativity is an important part of your process of self-understanding. Draw, paint, write, play an instrument, or act in a play—do whatever brings you joy. Take a class, go to a drumming ceremony, or buy a set of finger-paints and just have fun. Make a collage or weave a pot holder. Do it for yourself and keep doing it, and observe the joyful results.

Music

> *Music in balanced harmony is the song of the heavenly universes, manifested within the human earthly experience. With music, you can alter your state of mind and bring higher vibrations of light into your awareness.*
>
> —THE ANGELS

It would be difficult, if not impossible, to imagine a world without music. Music can enhance, even lift, our mood and cause our spirits to soar to heavenly realms. When we listen to various types of music, we have different responses. "Meditation" music stimulates peaceful feelings, "space" music activates the imagination, "rock" music or drumming may cause us to want to move our bodies in wild abandonment, and "classical" music puts us in touch with deeper aspects of emotion—all have been directly chan-neled from the One-Who-Created-Us-All. Listening to music gives us a deeper connection to the One and helps us expand our consciousness.

Why did the angels specifically refer to "*music in balanced harmony*" as having the ability to bring light to us? As stated earlier, we respond to different music from different places in ourselves. It is our experience that inharmonious music resonates with the parts of us that are confused and stuck. Thus it causes us to become more confused rather than giving us greater clarity, as other types of music can do.

Today we have many types of harmonious music to choose from. We suggest that you experiment with differ-ent kinds of music if you wish to test how these affect you. Also, do this whenever you are given the "Music" icon as your message while you are playing the game. This will also assist you in cleansing the emotional body and help you to integrate your personal attribute.

The Body

When one serves the temple (physical body) rather than the temple dweller (the spirit within the body) one cannot move or evolve into ascension. Would you tear up a temple of the One-Who-Creates-Us-All? Would you usurp the home of the same? You do. Drop your robes of defenses and accept the responsibility of choice in terms of what you put into your body-temple. It is important, Dear Ones, to have your attribute integrated into the body—your physical body. As the emotional body begins to purify, the physical body may feel sensations of discomfort as it adjusts to the trans-formation. Thus the body, as a communications temple of the living One, sends messages to your conscious awareness as to how the purification is proceeding. The healthier this body is, the easier it is for it to do this task and others.

—THE ANGELS

There is simply not enough space in this book to write about all the wisdom the angels shared with us about the care of the physical body. Suffice it to say that they stressed repeatedly that purification of the physical body is necessary in order to remember our true nature. They further and plainly spelled out to us that the body is the temple or vehicle through which we meet the One-Who-Created-Us-All, and thus, it should be treated with reverence and respect.

It was difficult for us, at first, to really comprehend the angels' messages at the beginning of this section. At the time, we were already working with our attributes, and this process had caused many of our emotional shadows to surface into the light. This alone was enough to handle, but to add to it the discipline of focusing on everything that went into our bodies seemed overwhelming. In the past, when each of us had tried to make major changes in how we cared for our bodies, we experienced a tremendous surge of emotional disruption. In retrospect, we now know it was because our unhealthy habits assisted in our denial of our shadow selves. It was easier to stuff unacceptable feelings than to acknowledge them. When we would attempt to break old habits, all that we had denied would come rising to the surface to be dealt with. Honestly, it was easier to return to the old bad habits.

But now we found ourselves in a double bind. While we desired purity with all of our hearts on the physical level, we were more than a little apprehensive about what we would have to go through in the process.

Nevertheless, like fools rushing in where angels feared to tread, together we jumped into our intention for purity and attempted to make the necessary changes in diet, etc., all at once. We have to confess: it didn't work. Each time feelings of anger, anxiety, depression, and other dark and shadowy aspects of ourselves would rise to the surface with great intensity, one would send us right back to a cigarette, or caffeine, or any of the other not-so-great substances that appeared to calm the emotional storm within us. Yet despite the fact that we knew we were participating in a temporary fix, we obviously weren't ready to change.

More than once, we went running to the angels for verbal assistance through the board. Each time they would gently remind us to let go of any guilt when we slipped up, to be easy on ourselves, to continue focusing on our attribute, and that intention alone would carry us through to our intended outcome. The changes would occur naturally, easily, and effortlessly if, they said, we would just do that one thing. Eventually as we began to surrender to the angels' point of view, lo and behold, they were once again right on target. Little by little, we began noticing a difference in what we were choosing to put into our bodies. The purer our bodies became, the easier it was to continue to deepen our experience of the "Initiation into Self."

As you continue focusing on your own attribute, you may find that you will, as a matter of course, begin to purify your body, too. The types of foods and other substances you put into your body will at first shift subtly—then, one day, you will notice that a dramatic transformation in the way you feed and nurture your physical body has taken place.

Don't forget that nurturing the physical body includes not only nourishing it with the right food but also permitting it physical expression. It is important to be attuned to your body's need for this expression. Any practice that encourages release of physical energy will help you to understand your body better and to integrate your attribute more fully. It will also help you to purge your emotional body, as it is particularly important in helping you to release your shadows, many of which have been residing in your body for quite some time. Any exercise or bodywork program is good: jogging, cycling, aerobics, swimming, yoga, dance, Tai Chi, or massage. As you progress in your chosen program and learn more about your own body, eating only healthy nutritious food and avoiding negative habits will become second nature to you. Pursue a program of health and exercise whenever, as you play the game, the angels have indicated "The Body" icon.

Summary

If you follow the lessons in this chapter, you will learn as we did, step-by-step, how to master communication with the angels through the process that they call an "Initiation into Self." This journey begins with your request to purify your emotional body, so you might communicate more easily with the Angelic Kingdom and perceive your world anew. You also learn to set an intention for clearing your old perceptual patterns by choosing to receive the angels' gifts—your very own special attribute. Next, you spend some time in thought considering and responding to questions from the angels, designed to help you deepen your understanding. Then you might move on to experiment with expanding your awareness and to applying your gift through journaling, meditation, dreamwork, nature, art, and music. Along the way, you learn about the importance of purifying and nurturing your physical body. Additionally, while working with these angelic assignments, you may become aware of parts of yourself that you previously denied or just plain didn't like. The necessity to accept and release these shadows is embraced.

Perhaps as you play *The Angels Talk,* the angels will give you further instructions for your special adventure. For us, the angels' "Initiation into Self" transformed our lives on every level, and we believe that these changes will continue into our future. We can only pray that your life will be similarly enriched, and that together we will—through our mutual intentions—co-create Heaven-on-Earth!

Section Two

*

Stories from the Angels

Chapter Three

Eden: Life in the Garden

*W*e are honored to introduce Section Two of this book, for it was only after we finished our "homework assignments"—writing our chapters of the book—that the angels would keep their promise to give us their story. While we plodded along the path to this end, we felt much like mules with carrots dangling in front of our faces, teasing us to take yet another step. At last, when they finally began to spell out their story, we were more than ready to receive our long-awaited gift. We must say, and we're sure you'll agree, that it was well worth the wait!

In the beginning, there was only the One, and the One, in a desire for companionship, breathed a grand cosmic exhalation. Instantly a great and vast void was filled with an infinite number of universes, including the one where this story takes place. Waves of creative energy emanated from the One and formed limitless numbers of dimensions. Out of these dimensions, a myriad of distinct individual souls emerged and, thus, all kingdoms were born in spirit, at once, to be companions to the Great-One-Who-Created-Us-All.

Every creation in this cosmic relationship, from the greatest to the least, **equally** embodied a perfect likeness of the One. This truth expressed the One and only eternally immutable Universal Law: we are all one! Another common trait of the new creations, from the largest to the smallest, was that each was endowed with unique individual laws or "patterns." The purpose of these patterns, which we can liken to a type of "spiritual DNA," was to ensure the structure and continuity of this newly forming masterpiece of divine art. These laws or patterns connected and related those of a similar nature, and with the creations they supported, a grand cosmic tapestry was thus woven.

The Angelic and Human Kingdoms originally had a lot in common, and we were fully conscious of each other as universal brothers and sisters who danced together in the light of the love flowing out from the One-Who-Gave-Birth-to-Us-All. Interestingly, both kingdoms were gifted by the One with special soul attributes, and both gleefully expressed these holy qualities in their mutual worlds. We angels were further given the responsibility for holding firmly in place, the framework, law, or patterning of these sacred attributes, unerringly, perfectly, and completely, to keep these patterns structured for you and for others. As if we were not already full of abundant possibilities, both kingdoms were also given the awe-inspiring gift of free will. While our soul's patterning was such that this gift was limited to a one-time decision, or use of free will, the gift to humans was to be an ongoing experience of free will, an exhilarating adventure in creativity.

Ultimately we were charged with a glorious cooperative opportunity: to assist **through our intention** in the evolution and development of a vastly diverse and beautiful garden paradise. And when our assignment was carried out to a certain extent, your kingdom would be given an extraordinary inheritance: that of caretaking the new garden, as if it were your very own. The planetary home of this blissful place was a "soul" who would come to be known to you as Earth, your most precious mother of three-dimensional life.

It is important to understand that none of the beings involved in this momentous project had, as yet, taken on physical forms **as they are currently understood.** At the time, your role was to populate, enjoy, explore and take care of the physical world; to be in it, not of it. Though you were not yet with a physical body, plans were being made and patterns for the emerging material plane of existence were beginning to take shape.

We gave our efforts fully and completely within the confines of time and space, cause and effect, and the other laws of our local universe, its dimensions and those of Earth. Each one of us endeavored in perfect unison so that the planet would evolve in perfect harmony, providing a physical home for its "children." And there arose from this activity a symphonic sound that further forged the connection between our two kingdoms, and this vibration was woven into the life of the planet. All the while, as we were engrossed in the creative spirit of cooperation on Earth, we all expressed our individual attributes perfectly.

We celebrated constantly as we held to our intention of planetary cooperation, and observed the results——the creative dance of the four elements of form: fire, earth, air, and water. As the sun rose and set upon each earthly day, the early skies in the newly forming atmosphere were awesomely beautiful. The colors of those primal sunrises and sunsets were vivid, with bright hues of contrasting purples, reds, pinks, and oranges. They provided a dazzling backdrop to the floating, shimmering clouds laden with moisture and heading to some destination whose thirst was in need of quenching.

The waters of Earth were immense, their greens and blues covered a great portion of your precious mother, nourishing each and every part of her with their life-giving qualities. In the sunlight, these waters sparkled with what appeared to be flawless diamonds sprinkled upon their surfaces. The vast oceans, smaller bays, rivers, and streams flowed across the land masses, making exquisite designs all over the new planet.

The air was richly filled with an effusion of nourishing gases; and on the ground, vegetation multiplied at an expeditious rate. The varieties of plants, trees, and grasses were incalculable, as the surface of your new home was quite literally bursting with life. Insects, fishes, birds, and mammals were, for the first time, moving about the Earth, and all rejoiced at the absolute perfection of the harmonious dance of life on the planet. The will of the One-Who-Created-Us-All had become a physical reality. Eden was ready for the Human Kingdom to be enjoyed as a direct experience, and so you began to settle into your new garden paradise, Heaven-on-Earth.

Just as the One-Who-Created-Us-All desired companionship, so did the One provide the Human Kingdom with the same desire. Thus, from each soul emerged yet another soul, one who would be equal and yet opposite in appreciable ways for the sake of diversity. These "twin souls" were called male and female, and like all Creation, each one adhered to the primary Universal Law that we are all One. And so, these companion souls were lovely complements for one another, and they were happy. In addition, each couple had fellow sojourners: a pair of angels who had the same soul attributes. These angels would be guiding lights for the pair's experience, and later, as their role became more of a protective one, they came to be known as your Guardian Angels. They are still with you today.

The Human and Angelic Kingdoms worked hand in hand, constantly communicating telepathically with one another and all other earthly life. It was through our free-will choices to align with the One that we knew each other utterly and absolutely. Each group of humans and angels was given a particular focus within the magnificent Eden—one in which they could best use their attributes in their respective roles as caretaker and explorer. There were those who studied the dynamics of the density of physical matter: the scientific structures of how each element (fire, earth, air, and water) developed into various forms. These souls worked in unison, through their intention, to help stabilize these material formations. There were other individual groups who were artistically creative and worked with weaving radiant colors and natural design into the developing tapestry of life. Still, there were others who could be likened to historians, recording each and every happenstance of the Earth experience upon the Universal Records of Creation. Then there were those who cared for the sounds and vibrations emanating to and from our garden world. Assisting the mineral, plant, and animal kingdoms to evolve into their highest and best potentials was another area of focus, as was helping to maintain a balance in the patterns of temperature and weather. Again the possibilities were limitless. There are simply no words to describe the perfect harmony in which this unfolding reality was taking place!

At this point in our story, we will focus our narrative upon two individual souls known to you as Adam and Eve. We do this in order to personalize our tale for your human comprehension of events that unfolded in our idyllic paradise garden home.

As you may have guessed through our description of life in Eden, Adam and Eve were able to move about with just their "intention" to do so, and consequently, in this way, they explored the many wonders to behold in the new garden. They marveled at the tiny crabs scuttling about the sandy beaches by the seas. The antics of the monkeys who inhabited the great jungles made them laugh, and they marveled at how the smaller fish "talked" when the greater fish swam close by. They were exhilarated at the massive mountains of ice at either end of the Earth, while the tropical rain forests held a particular fascination for the couple, and they took pleasure in exploring the flora and fauna found in them. It was here, where they spent most of their time, that they assisted through their will in the development of species conducive to rain-forest life. They were together, happy, and filled with joy as they accomplished their tasks. With their entire beingness, they were able to experience an indescribable bliss as they fulfilled their individual missions.

The enrapturing love that was present in the Garden of Eden so permeated each and every atom of physical life that, if you could only recall the memory of it for a second, your future would be transformed instantly; your awareness would purify in a split second, and you would once again return to Heaven-on-Earth.

Chapter Four

The Descent into Matter

*I*n the beginning of Adam and Eve's sojourn upon Earth, life was different than it is in your present awareness. Among those in your kingdom, there did not exist any sense of "separation" from the will of the One. Sentiments or attitudes such as negativity, hatred, fear, violence, shame, guilt, anger, sadness, frustration, or resistance were not present. As we depicted in the previous chapter, life was gloriously created out of the pure and unconditional love of the One, and this was perfectly expressed in the Garden of Eden for many eons.

It is here that we must temporarily digress in order to explain what transpired within the realm of angels before the Earth was created and humanity entertained the choice to descend into matter. We want to share these experiences with you so you can more fully comprehend the relationship between our two kingdoms. As our story continues to unfold, you will see that we, too, had a choice to descend from a state of Divine Intent.

As we have already explained, among the unique patterns and gifts given to the Angelic Kingdom was the one-time gift of free will. As this was bequeathed by the One, so was it received by all angels. The most beautiful angel, known to you as Lucifer, was the first angelic being to purposefully investigate the potential of free will. In fact, he became so thoroughly enchanted at the prospect of traveling the universe according to his own personal aspirations that he began to disregard the will of the One. It was through Lucifer's **intention alone** that the underlying reality of his desires was made manifest. So he was released unto his self-created choice of self-indulgence and separation. Having made his one-time free-will choice, Lucifer was unable to return to his original state of being. In truth, he could not even contemplate the possibility of a return, simply because this was no longer possible within the framework of the gift or patterning. Quite simply, Lucifer, through his own doing, was stuck with the assignment of self-importance. As he opened the doorway to this new reality, many other angels used their one-time free-will decision to follow in his footsteps. And thus, these legions of aberrant angels have traveled the universe expressing their attributes of selfishness and separateness, holding perfectly to the pattern of their choices, wherever allowed. As you read on, you will understand the connection between these events, which took place within the Angelic Kingdom, and how they related to your own descent into the material world.

Suffice it to say, the greater majority of the angels chose to adhere to the guiding light of the One. It was these loving angels who were related with the developing souls within your own Human Kingdom. These were the angels who joyfully assisted in the co-creation of the beautiful garden paradise that came to be your home. By virtue of the purity of intent that our two kingdoms held sacred in the formation of the planet Earth, it was simply inconceivable that Lucifer and his legions could become a part of our new world. The framework of our own laws of operation did not provide an opening for connecting with their dissimilar laws of self-important intentions. Life developed in a perfectly splendid manner upon the blessed Earth.

As we rejoin Adam and Eve in the lush tropical rain forest,

the unfolding drama of creation was still being fully enjoyed. Everywhere the couple turned, the rich diversity of life forms provided a never-ending array of entertainment, and Adam and Eve delighted in every moment of their time spent in the garden forest. Their companion angels likewise joined in their merriment, and the blissful ecstasy could have perhaps continued for what might have been an eternity. But then, all of it changed. . . .

You see, Adam and Eve were fully aware of their special gift of free will, and knew they could instantly direct their unfettered intentions into any pursuit that interested them. In this way they, along with their companion angels, cooperated fully with the One in bringing the glory of heaven to Earth. Over time, and much like Lucifer of our own Angelic Kingdom, Adam and Eve became more and more enchanted with the framework of free will and matter, and the gifts of the material world.

As the couple directed an ever-increasing focus upon these gifts, they began to turn their attention away from the actual Creator of all of the gifts. Their companion angels knew precisely what was happening, because they had witnessed it before with Lucifer. They knew Adam and Eve were beginning to erringly exercise free will, and they reminded the couple that it was the desire of the One that they were to be on the Earth, not of it. Since the angels loved their brother and sister unconditionally, they also communicated to Adam and Eve that if they were to pursue this developing intention to self-indulge in the material plane of Earth, their lives would be altered forever, the Human Kingdom's freedom would be lost. Humanity would then become subject to the laws or patterning of matter itself and, therefore, would come to know a world of duality: light and dark, hot and cold, love and fear, etc. Additionally, like Lucifer, they would be forced by the gift of free will to live out the fulfillment of their choice. In their precious childlike innocence,

Adam and Eve could not even begin to comprehend the meaning of their companion angels' important message.

The seeds of curiosity continued to grow and take root within the patterning of Adam and Eve's will. Eventually these seeds grew into a fully desired self-centered intention to experience matter. Instantly the patterning of their will shifted its shape, and simultaneously a door opened for similar patterns to enter into the garden. This single event of misdirected intentions gave Lucifer and his legions the opportunity to directly and willfully experience relationships within the Human Kingdom. These disheartening angels were only too delighted at the opportunity to infiltrate Eden. With the encouragement and support of these self-seeking angels who were seasoned in the ways of self-indulgent living, Adam and Eve **chose to act** upon their willful intentions. Their companion angels stood by, helplessly observing what was to become one of the most significant events to occur in human evolution—yet "devolution" might be a more appropriate term.

Adam and Eve moved about the garden, excited at the prospect of experiencing physicality. With their gift of free will, they were actually capable of altering their own luminous shapes into physical bodies. To cause this transformation, the pair simply focused the desire upon their energetic patterning and intended to merge with material form. At once, their wish was granted. They admired their newly created material bodies and were amazed at the differences between them. Like the animals, their male and female characteristics had also materialized.

As a result of this self-indulgent choice, the five senses— seeing, hearing, smell, taste, and touch—sprang forth from their broken will, and they were able to discern their environment only in these five "separate" ways. Before the momentous choice, they perceived the garden paradise with their entire beingness, rather than through separate senses. They were astonished by all of the unique sensations they were receiving through their new forms. In their Earth bodies, they could feel the leaves crunching on the woodland floor beneath their feet as they took each step. They could hear the symphony of the forest sounds—birds chirping, tree branches rustling against one another in the warm breezes, dragonflies buzzing about their heads. Each new thing to look at was a delight, while exotic aromas permeated their nostrils. Finally Adam and Eve wanted to experience the sensation of taste. They spotted a delectable fruit hanging from a tree in the very center of the forest. They plucked it from a branch, split it in half, and each took a big, crunchy bite. The succulent fruit and its delicious juices filled their mouths with sweetness. With each act of absorbing the patterns of matter into their senses, they noticed not only that their bodies were becoming more "dense," but that they were also encoded with patterns quite unlike those they were normally accustomed to, those that had not received the gift of free will. They wanted both worlds and could let go of neither.

Unlike Lucifer and his followers, who only had a one-time gift of free will, Adam and Eve could shift back and forth between the Law of the One and the laws of duality; however, the purity and ease with which they were able to do this lessened with each go-around. They didn't pay attention to this, though, and at long last, they shifted their focus once more toward recapturing their previous state of being. They had a stunning surprise awaiting them. The new material patterns that had become so much a part of them were not programmed for free will, and having mixed with them, the ability to use their weakened will to easily shift their patterning was becoming mysteriously complex and difficult. Try as they might, the couple simply could not reenter their previous state of purity, innocence, and oneness. Adam and Eve called upon their companion angels for help, but to no avail. Like lost sheep, they couldn't find their *way. Not even their special friends could assist. For within the angelic structure, the angels could not interfere with the free-will choices of their dearest friends of the Human Kingdom. Other than holding true to their angelic purpose, there was not much they could do. The angels could only continue to love and protect their human counterparts and perfectly maintain the patterns of their mutual attributes, until the two discovered the way to recover their lost paradise.*

Adam and Eve began to feel limited and ashamed of themselves. They started to argue and blamed themselves and each other for the choice they had made. With their divided senses, they had begun to perceive a realm of separation, struggle, and opposition. They had lost the "key" to paradise and had fully entered the world of duality. Adam and Eve's innocent intentions had begun in a "twinkling of an eye," and yet so far-reaching were the effects of their choices nothing could undo what had been done. The only remnant of their perfect state was the beckoning of the One's intent, constantly calling them to return to their true home. The angels of light unerringly carried this message to human souls all over Earth, and this divine message has been received by humanity as an inner hunger for something so close, yet so far away. Humanity has been searching to satisfy the hunger ever since. Little did they know, the key to their return to Heaven-on-Earth lay within their own hearts, awaiting recovery.

Even though we have presented this story as if it pertained to two individuals, know that the choice to merge with matter spread instantly and simultaneously like wildfire throughout the Human Kingdom. The content of the matter that each individual chose to explore differed, but the context was always the same: willfully intending to explore the framework of the three-dimensional world. The divine intent of the One-Who-Created-

Us-All was relegated to the back burner while humanity was lost in self-indulgence and disconnection.

As human beings became more entrenched in the material world, they also became more sensitive to its patterns. Insects would come to feed upon their bodies, and animals they had played with only a short time before would seek them out as prey. Sometimes they found themselves shivering in the snow, and other times, baking under the hot sun. Their paradise had become a hostile place to live, completely opposite from their original experience. They had to make clothing to cover their bodies and build shelters to further protect themselves from the elements that had once been friends. Their encounters with physical reality were bringing to the surface of their awareness all sorts of judgments and new beliefs about life. Fear, doubt, mistrust, and other dark shadows of their former selves created a veil within them. This veil of distorted perceptions dropped over their "emotional bodies," the subtle body that was the link between themselves, their angels, and their Source, further disabling their conscious connection with the One-Who-Created-Us-All. Their memories of the garden paradise of Eden were fast fading into a vague dream, something they couldn't quite remember.

As self-importance became the law of the land, people who were developing physical power began treating those with other intentions disrespectfully. Males fought and warred with other males. Females, who were physically smaller and weaker, were subjugated to an altogether lesser position in the developing societies. Women also expressed and held the patterns for the feminine aspects of the One, including the seeds for creative possibilities. Because it was out of these seeds that the intention for exploring materiality arose, men blamed women for their predicament and refused to listen to them on any matter. Women grew resentful of the male dominant force and chose to undermine their men in subtle ways—thus a vicious cycle between the opposite sexes began. They didn't realize that all humans were blessed with masculine and feminine qualities, and that the choice of one is the choice of all. Or that honoring the feminine aspects of humanity might give birth to the possibility of returning home—and that honoring the male aspects would support the strength needed for action to carry out the task. By treating each other in a contemptuous manner, the men and women were simply mirroring their own disgust for themselves. Only when both sexes discovered once again the importance of truly honoring each other, and all life, for that matter, would the chance for redemption be available.

Since there was so much unrest and fear among individuals, people began to band together in groups—some for protection and some to gain power over those less fortunate. These latter groups grew in force by holding the land hostage. Governments were formed in order to control the growing masses of people; false laws and regulations were created, and the masses were commanded to follow them or endure unspeakable suffering. Money was developed for trading and for fulfilling physical desires and was controlled by those who came to power. The people who didn't have power in the physical reality were forced to work long and hard hours, so that they were too tired and weak to redirect their attention toward the ever-present mysterious calling of their hearts. For the meek, just surviving the harsh realities of daily living was a major feat. Their creative juices were running dry, and no one, not the meek, nor the strong, was happy. The Human Kingdom was indeed experiencing Hell-on-Earth—or, another opposite in the world of duality. The angels of light presented themselves whenever possible, but to no avail. The Human Kingdom could no longer sense their relationship with the loving unseen beings.

There were very, very few who were able to withstand the

strengthening forces of Lucifer's misguided angels and their fellow humans. Most also eventually succumbed to material desires, as they tried to assist their fellow human beings out of the willful predicament. But there were some individuals who chose to remain true to the intent of the One-Who-Created-Us-All. These special souls steadfastly focused with all their will upon the primary Universal Law of One, and over time, they were able to express the light of our Creator into the world as master teachers.

One thing that those in power could do nothing about was the quiet but powerful presence of the One, lovingly calling all children of Earth home once again. Even though this calling was heard only as a silent whisper, it was unwavering. This truth remained solidly ever-present, like a dormant seed in the hearts of all human beings. Yet, because of the veil, no one could sense the yearning clearly enough to discern its message. There was just a constant nagging desire for something better. Those in power created false religions around the master teachers to placate and control the growing numbers of people. While the foundations of these faiths were based on the Universal Law of One, dogmatic doctrines built upon the cornerstones of truth, they were structured so that the congregations of these religions could only fall deeper into the mire of disillusionment and matter. Thus many human souls came to be temporarily controlled by those who demanded allegiance, granting themselves authority over your kingdom. Even when we angels were able to appear through the purity of a human's heart and will, to bring an important message, those in power would use the loving event to support their own end. Their distorted ability to "reason" twisted the true nature of life in a great variety of ways. They had made sure their power would not be usurped. Unconditional love, acceptance, and joy on Earth was impossible to reach, given the false maps to this end. These so-called

65

leaders were not to blame. They were simply ignorant. The dual nature of the human victims/manipulators was simply two sides of the same coin, that of choosing the laws of matter rather than the Law of One.

And so it came to be true that the Human Kingdom descended into matter through the use of free-will choice. All the while, we of the Angelic Kingdom, your brothers and sisters of light, have waited patiently, carrying the patterns of your soul attributes, and praying that you would soon open your hearts with the key of unconditional loving intent, unlock the door to the Divine Will of the One, and begin your homeward-bound return. Miraculously, not long ago, an event occurred that stimulated a spiritual revolution, whereupon an "ascension" to remembering yourselves was initiated, and our prayers and messages entered once again into your awareness. Our story continues. . . .

Chapter Five

The Ascension

*A*lthough the Human Kingdom was given the ongoing gift of free will, this gift was confined within the boundaries of local Universal Laws. One of these laws was that the Human Kingdom could and would not be allowed to destroy Earth, much less the entire universe. When a device such as a nuclear bomb detonates, the resulting chain reaction tears at the fabric of the Universal Design. Thus, in your 1940s, when those who pretended to govern the people of Earth created this weapon to wreak mass destruction upon the planet, something had to be done. Therefore, with a divine directive emanating from the will of the One, the Earth's energy field was thoroughly drenched with a flood of light-wave patterning, and this re-vised the prevailing laws of the Angelic and Human King-doms. Primarily, the patterning permeated human souls, yet to be born, with an intention to ascend in their hearts and minds to a renewed desire for recovering their lost garden paradise and the Law of One. In other words, the One, through loving grace, fortified the will of humankind with light. Certain angels were also encouraged to merge their own elevated pat-terns of light with the newly implanted human souls. This was something that had previously been outside the parameters of *the kingdoms' laws. These changes drastically altered the "spiritual DNA" of the future children of Earth. Thus every baby born after the first atomic explosion became an Earth Angel, and this is true. Alas, when they were born into their Earth bodies, they temporarily forgot their mission as the veil of distorted perceptual filters descended upon them. These souls as children grew up in what appeared to be idyllic environments, and many were trusting and open enough in their awareness to be able to actually "see" their companion angels. They were happy in their innocence, and life seemed to be unfolding perfectly according to plan.*

When the children grew up, many of them were sent away to a war, and few could reason why. When graphic scenes of the horrible carnage were seen on television by the ones left at home, their forgotten purpose to bring the light-filled intention of the One-Who-Creates-Us-All into Earth was, at long last, remembered. At once, these souls began to speak out of Divine Intention and soon came to be appropriately known as "flower children." They preached free love, peace, and joy for all living things. They turned their backs on the illusions of money, power, and war, and encouraged all to seek a greater spiritual reality. It was as if a light had been turned on, and indeed "One" had.

In some ways, the flower children mimicked life in the garden. In a childlike manner, they played music and danced in the streets. They took to parks and forests in large numbers and began to better appreciate the animals, plants, rocks, and things of the natural world. Each Earth Angel had his/her special purpose for assisting the Human Kingdom in finding a way to the light, a way to remember the soul's attribute. Some brought the centering practices of meditation and yoga to mass consciousness. Others brought forth the teachings of the masters. Still others worked fervently in helping the creatures of the nature kingdoms, by giving them a voice. Some assisted in bringing awareness of the Angelic Kingdom to Earth. Additionally, there were those who brought alternative healing methods or the way of "right livelihood" to the people. Yes, these Earth Angels held the pattern for the inward return home in countless ways, and all of the children together created bridges for crossing from the place of duality and separation to the land of Heaven-on-Earth. We, of the Angelic Kingdom, rejoiced in the realization of your Human Kingdom.

Deep within the very essence of the Earth Angels' hearts rested the knowledge that the kingdom of heaven was truly within, and that the intention to know this truth was the key to the door to paradise. In addition, they were also aware that what would turn the key would be unconditional love, and further, that this love began with the love of the true Self. In order to develop this state of being, humanity would first have to recover its original purpose. If humankind could only learn to truly remember Eden and recognize that there was no original sin, only innocence, the door to the garden would unlock and swing wide open, beckoning the Human Kingdom's return to love.

This journey home has brought the shadows of illusion to the surface of human consciousness. Everything not of pure, simple, beautiful truth is being exposed for what it is—a yearning for love in all the wrong places. The shadows have been present all along, but humanity, in a state of shame, could not bear to look at them. It has just been too painful to love that which has been judged ugly and despicable, especially if the struggle is a deeply personal one. Still, the light has been turned on, and there is no choice but to move according to the deepest inner calling of the soul. Many of you observe with horror as violence, drug and alcohol addiction, abject poverty, terrifying diseases, and a potential for nuclear, biological, and environmental catastrophe threaten life. There can no longer be any denial of the overindulgence with the substance of matter. Becoming hostage to the god of money has greatly complicated human lives. Government, some churches, courts, and other authorities of false law are exposed by the daily media as corrupt. Even on a personal level, self-importance rises like a ghostly specter—of life lived as death. No one has been left untouched by the shadows of illusion. The response for everyone has been the same: perceptually distorted and shadowy emotions of fear, rage, resistance, doubt, shame, and guilt.

What is wonderful is that eventually everyone will quickly tire of blaming each other and even Self! For all that has to be done is to accept the shadows for what they are—past choices—and send them into the Light. Then focus on your newly remembered intention, that of cooperation through love, with Self, others, and, most importantly, with the One-Who-Created-Us-All. All the while, hold fast to the art of letting go of what is no longer important to you.

Step by step, you will more clearly realize the need for simplicity and inner peace. Amazingly, just by intending to heal your soul's purpose, incredible things will begin to happen. For it is true that the way to ascend within your hearts and minds to Heaven-on-Earth is simply through the constant and un-erring intention to do so. You will once again return to Eden in the same manner through which you left, through your special gift of free will, and enter into harmony with all life. By focus-ing on the intention of the highest and best attributes of the One-Who-Created-Us-All, the ability to do the same will expand. You will then move fully into the promised ascension of humankind.

The ascension is simply the awareness or the recognition of the intent of the One, and allowing that recognition to lift you into a joyful place. The promise of the One is that you will begin to lighten, to be less "dense" and less attached to the world of matter. You will once again be in the Earth, not of it. You will find yourself moving with complete knowing—with the knowledge of creativity, joy, love, peace, and laughter, too! Ecstasy will be expressed fully on the Earth once again. You will again have total awareness of your purpose and patterning.

Do not worry yourselves about the shadows; just as the descent began with an intention, and then spread, so will the process of ascension. The will to align with Divine Intent is imbued with great power that can reunite all and usurp all illusion. The intent through that focus will grow and grow, and all of the aspects of your life shall come into harmony once again.

Lastly, remember that it is of utmost importance to apply your intentions of re-union into your daily lives, so that other humans will take notice and develop in a similar manner. The more often you reach out to assist others, the more quickly the ascension will occur for all.

The Angels of Light will help and encourage this process. Lucifer and his minions will go elsewhere, waiting for a graceful return to the One. Together, let all of us, Human and Angelic Kingdom alike, re-create Heaven-on-Earth through the ascension from matter into the One-Who-Created-Us-All!

Chapter Six

Answers from the Angels

Each of you would do well to focus deeply on questions you would like to ask us: questions about the Angelic Kingdom, questions for which you have a burning desire to know the answer. Consider that you have the ability to sit down with us in the flesh to talk normally. What would you want to know about us? Ask in ten different ways that which would have your desire for knowledge fulfilled.

—The Angels

$\mathcal{A}$s we became more familiar with the mechanics of how to play the game, we began spending a portion of each of our weekly board sessions asking the angels all the things we ever wanted to know about—everything from whether or not angels have wings to more personal questions about our journey of initiation. One day, much to our delight, they asked us to put our incessant curiosity to work and make a list of all the questions we would ask the angels as if they were sitting before us in the flesh. This chapter is the result.

We hope you find the answers as fascinating and thought-provoking as we did.

1. How do the angels perceive the human kingdom?

Humankind was created as spirit in the physical world with the spice of free will. This creation allowed you to freely experience whatever was or is able to be manifested within a particular framework. Over time, humanity chose to explore the corner of the framework that is the illusion of the veil. Within that choice, humanity became lost and began believing it was, or is, the only world.

It is into this self-created manifestation that we are moving—to assist humanity in remembering the truth. We find humans are extraordinary in their ability to find and direct the free-will intention into a thing that can only bring more misery. You are, as a race, stuck in a mire of self-choosing, and that choice has possibly brought you to a point of no return. By this we mean that humanity has threatened life as you know it on Earth. However, humanity will not be allowed to destroy the universe, and this is so. We love you and, with other beings, are doing everything in our power to assist. Further, we perceive you with unconditional love and see through the illusion.

2. If the angels could communicate one thing to humanity, what would it be?

We are one. We are all one! If you want to know why or how, imagine what life on Earth would be like if this were realized. There would simply be no separation between any thing, person, place, creation, etc. Only unity, safety, peace, etc. No politics, religion, sex, race, age, separation, etc. Try it on. We are one moving and expressing through the framework of duality. We are **in** *this world, not* **of** *it.*

3. Please tell us anything that would assist us in understanding the Law of One.

This is law, the law, and it is the first Universal Law. All other laws spring forth from this truth. Consider the essential essence of this law in every thought and action. Consider what life would be like if all of the Human Kingdom practiced this law with full consciousness. Think upon it! Continually!

4. When we ask for angelic assistance, what do you do?

We do much. First, there is our presence. Second, there is our intent. Third, there is the work we perform on the energy body. We assist in healing and bringing balance into the energy body by using light waves and prayer. This becomes more powerful according to the intent of the human who allows and accepts our assistance.

5. Are angels always with us?

Always!

6. Do angels come whenever we ask?

Yes, always.

7. Are there guidelines for angels to follow when assisting humans?

Yes. We have a wide-open carte blanche, a directive from the Father-Mother Spirit, yet we must work in accordance with a soul's blueprint or pattern. This is true with any life form we assist and guide.

8. Can angels assist us with anything we ask?

Yes.

9. What is the most important thing a human can do to accept and become more aware of the angelic influence?

*Intend it! Believe and expect you will know us. We communicate directly to your inner senses, and yes, there has been an angel or two who has become frustrated with not being heard. So believe and listen and do not discount the voices, visions, feelings within, for if you accept and believe, you can also know it is us. We always come. We are **not** always acknowledged.*

10. What would you like humans to realize most about the Angelic Kingdom?

How close we are in our patterning. Knowing that we are all one and that we both have bodies of light will free you of doubt, fear, and other painful aspects of life on present-day Earth. We are so very close.

11. Describe a normal angelic life.

The normal angelic life is the very same as the normal human life. It is a glorious life filled with grace, love, and joy. It is one in which, through the wish of our Creator, we express an unparalleled adventure. We frolic and play, learn and discover the great treasures of the universe. This is accomplished in a timely fashion within the laws of our respective kingdoms and within the context of Universal Law.

12. Could you explain the purpose of Guardian Angels?

Guardian Angels are those who hold the soul or spirit pattern of the individual to the Throne of Grace. This is always true. They assist, guide, and teach, with respect to the calling, from the place of purity and knowing within each soul's center. When one's consciousness aligns with their soul's vibration, the

Guardian Angel takes on a more developed role. The angel is then able to connect more deeply with the purpose within its own pattern. One can then directly contact this being and develop at a higher frequency. The Guardian Angel is your connection with spirit, as the divine pattern unfolds from a point within your being to the rest of creation. Angels of this nature guide, protect, and connect.

13. Do we have the same Guardian Angel all our lives?

Most of the time, if there is a major shift in the life path, there will be an exchange in the Guardian Angel. The shift may be one that alters the life path, such as an accident or a serious illness. We would say to you that these come about when a soul chooses to move in opposition to his or her original pattern or design. A new design is then programmed into the soul, requiring a different Guardian Angel—however, not always.

14. Does our Guardian Angel look like us?

No. But there are similar aspects in your energetic makeup, a connecting link between life forms.

15. How can I recognize my Guardian Angel in my dreams?

Look. Look with your intention. Be open. Expect. Experience. Believe. It is simple, simple, simple. However, if you are looking for an experience that will only satisfy your senses, with that intent, you may diminish the experience that is possible when recognition occurs through your inner being.

16. Do guardian angels choose which humans they will assist?

The choice belongs to both. It is not one-sided.

17. Do we have more than one Guardian Angel?
Depends. In most cases, no.

18. When we die, do our Guardian Angels go with us?
Yes, for a short period.

19. Do our pets have Guardian Angels?
Yes. All physical life forms have Guardian Angels. These angels hold the holy pattern of the form to our Creator, and they guide, protect, and so on.

20. What is the specific relationship between the Human and the Angelic Kingdoms?
We are one! We are one!

21. What is the difference between the Human and Angelic Kingdoms?
The Angelic Kingdom carries forth Universal Law by assisting with forming kingdoms, and we also hold the pattern for the various kingdoms. The Human Kingdom represents an experiment of spirit in physical manifestation.

22. Do angels have wings?
Only in the mind of the perceiver. We are light-energy beings.

23. Does our space program interfere with angels in any way?
Yes. The technology of your present program is in conflict with the physics of the type of patterning within and without your own atmosphere. One day this program will be history;

space exploration will be more aligned with Universal Law. There are those beings, both from our kingdom and other kingdoms or civilizations, who are directly and indirectly working with this situation.

24. Are angels male or female?
Both and neither. We recognize the Law of One and embody the same. This includes gender, or the illusion of such.

25. Who gives angels their assignments and why?
The One-Who-Is-at-the-Source-of-All-Life. We assist in the development of different life forms, assist those in remembering the One. We light up the path or the way home and are the keepers of Universal Law. We guard the sacred, make it easy to know and to remember. Also, we are to be a connecting link between life forms and spirit. We are assigned our attributes through our will, which is in alignment with the One.

26. What kind of bodies do angels have?
Light! Light! Light! We are, as are all, a form of energy designed by our Creator.

27. How do angels decide how they will communicate with humans?
It depends upon the calling from the place of purity and knowing within each soul's center; and then we have a certain amount of freedom as to how to bring this about, which aligns with the will, awareness, and beliefs of each human.

28. Do angels have friends?
Yes, all. And we do, depending on circumstance, radiate more completely with those who are connected with our purpose.

29. Where do angels go when they are finished with their assignments?

It depends on several things. Some move to other assignments. Others choose to take a break and bask in the glory of another place and time, in a manner of speaking.

30. Do angels have feelings?

Not in the way humans do. We have states of being that could be labeled as emotions, such as joy, happiness, love, peace, and abundance, etc.

31. How many angels are there?

Countless. Countless. Countless.

32. How big is an angel?

Infinitesimal to infinitely large.

33. Can you help students with their tests?

You must meet us halfway. Let those who would call upon us expect assistance. However, we, the Angelic Kingdom and the Human Kingdom, work together. We cannot take responsibility from you. We can lighten the load. We can assist you with your studies and guide you through doors we open, but you have to meet us in these endeavors.

34. Do angels have soul mates?

Yes. Each form has an equal half. When these portions are rejoined, the truth of the One becomes fulfilled in the union. These so-called other halves have been named at times "soul mates," and they possess similar qualities and purpose.

35. What do angels like best about humans?

Your capacity for love.

36. How can humans help angels?

Through developing awareness of the truth. This means to become aware of individual purpose and, with that, connect with the Universal Law of One.

37. Do angels breathe?

Yes, energy and light. Drawing in that which energizes, and letting go of that which is to be returned to the One.

38. Do angels live forever?

Yes. Everyone lives forever. Sometimes we change forms, but we never change our essence. We can change form as law provides with a simple focus of intention. Some of us choose to take on a form of physicality that is greater or lesser in density. Some may explore worlds which have formations that are unique to you.

39. Why do angels seem to appear to some and not to others?

We appear to everyone. Sometimes soul-desire calls us forth to manifest more fully in the physical realm, and sometimes a person's awareness is altered so we may be seen. And then there are those who are more sensitive to our kingdom. This occurs simply through intention and is expressed through either the unconscious or conscious, or both. These "sensitives" are keenly aware of their inner senses, or intuition.

40. Do angels have pets?

No.

41. What makes a smiling angel so happy?

The One.

42. Do angels read books?

We do not read books. However, there are places of study. There are many great halls of learning, where vast amounts of knowledge are stored. These are most recognizable to you in their similarity to your libraries. We do inspire books and aid in the creation of these, though.

43. Do angels ever experience fear?

No. We are deeply connected with the Law of One.

44. What can we do to see or hear angels clearly?

Look and listen.

45. What would it take for everyone to see angels more clearly?

Awareness on the level of mass consciousness.

46. Why do some people seem to experience angels without asking?

It is important to know that we come when called from the will of the soul; but when that opportunity arises, one may not be consciously aware of the soul's call.

47. How do angels talk to each other?

Through vibration.

48. Can angels see God?

Everywhere. Can't you?

49. What color are angels?

All colors. We are light.

50. How are angels born?

Through the intent of God.

51. Do angels eat? If so, what?

In a manner of speaking, energy.

52. Do angels sleep?

Angels can rest or change activities.

53. Where do angels live?

It depends. Words are inadequate to perfectly describe that place. We live in a dimension of pure intent, and in this, there is perfect harmony in all respects of what you would term time and space. We live in refined and subtle light waves. We have structures, to be sure. These could be likened to some of your New Age artists' renditions of other dimensions. Travel is much simpler in this world, as are relationships and communications, because we are in harmony with the Law of One, and all is instantly at our call or desire. Even though, to humans, density appears more real, our world is pure light and seemingly subtle, but more imposing in its potency to create.

54. Do angels go to school?

Some, depending upon the purpose or life plan. Those studying the evolving sciences of life forms are an example. They study at angelic libraries, the Akashic halls of learning, which contain the knowledge of all life forms, history, future, etc. The Akashic is a term describing a portion of all that has, within it, the knowledge of all time and space. There are places where this knowing, this wisdom, is collected into a denser form, and this is where we can tap directly into these manifestations. The Akasha permeates into every atom and subatomic particle. It is everywhere at the disposal of those who would tap into it.

55. Do angels have likes and dislikes?

Angels have personalities and resonate with those of like

vibration. Some can be quite distinct in voicing their preference. Likes and dislikes do not adequately describe our attributes.

56. Do angels ever go on vacation?

We angels are given freedom beyond what may be considered. We are not puppets. Rather, we are the emissaries of God. This fact in no way hampers or restricts our freedom. It is exactly our gift from this source that gives us our freedom, while remaining true to the will of the One. This ability to move and choose freely is always in accord and with the Law of One, and we can and do choose to take vacations.

57. Can you give us a description of the angelic hierarchy?

*The structure of the angelic hierarchy, or levels, is in the mind of the beholder. The universal structure **appears** linear, or even hierarchical, from humanity's perception, but this is simply not true. When this illusion is dispelled, it changes the perception. This altered awareness allows one to open to the possibility of a mutually chosen life in the universe. There is only choice, and the choice is in accordance with the will of the One. There are those of us who have a larger portion of activity, and this would require a more powerful amount of energy to carry out the purpose, or assignment. There is no hierarchy, although there is the appearance of such.*

58. Do angels ever have problems?

No. Opportunities.

59. Do humans ever become angels?

Yes. Humankind evolved in several patterns. Some are patterned with that of the angelic, others with that of other civilizations of the universe. DNA is the first movement of energy or universal patterning to become manifest in the physical. The physical is a mirror of its spiritual design. So the design is sent forth through the movement of divine will and then becomes manifest as DNA structure. The form then emerges from this into physical form. This is further manipulated by the One. And at times, in the development of form, it is necessary to infuse one pattern with another or portions of another. Therefore, there are those on Earth whose DNA is infused with that of the Angelic Kingdom. And there are those who are infused with that of other kingdoms in the universe—i.e., Aucturians, Pleadians, or Sirian patterning, etc. This could be a book in itself.

60. Where do angels get their knowledge?

From the infusion and direction of spirit, where spirit is to be understood. Essentially all knowledge comes from the will of the One.

61. Do angels pray? If so, how?

Always. Alignment with the will of the One.

62. Do angels meditate? If so, how?

Ditto to the previous response.

63. Do angels really play musical instruments?

Yes. We align with vibrations and express them so they are heard throughout the heavens. We manifest at will, according to Universal Law. We are one. We create our instruments at will.

64. When was the first angel born?

You see, all life was intended in the same moment. We were created at the same time as all life. Since that moment, the creative design has carried on the plan of the universal livelihood.

65. Are the job descriptions of the angels changing, and are there more than we are aware of at present?

They are expanding. There are many more as yet unnamed angelic forms, or families. We could say, as you humans do, that we are all angels, and then we could further separate into categories, and further still into individuals. These categories cannot be counted in your system or your present level of understanding.

66. How many angels fit on the head of a pin?

It depends upon the form of energy the angels manifest. Countless, in their present ability.

67. Do all communications from the One have to come through intermediaries like the angels?

*No. The preferable direct experience with the Creator is constant, moment-to-moment experience throughout all of your perceptions. Direct experience is just as it states. We are but a portion of what is in this answer. There is no hierarchy, so you can and do access the One directly. We **assist.** You receive communications of spiritual nature through many means, such as through other people, art, nature, events, etc. The One is everywhere. This is a limitless universe.*

68. Are angels the only ones who act as delegates for the One?

No, we are all emissaries. We are those who would move in complete harmony with Universal Law. There are others such as devas, elementals, etc., whose mission is more specific to a plane of operation. We are also a connecting link between worlds, as well as what has already been given. There are also light travel-

ers who can traverse dimensions. We work in harmony with these, as well as galactic builders, star souls, etc.

69. How can we know the difference between communications from the angels and communications from other beings?

*You **know**. There are no impure sensations or fears within your experience when communing with us. You are as children in your response, and you know you are secure. There is an energy of playfulness.*

70. How can we learn to see you?

Intention. Awareness. Dreaming. Meditation. As your development increases, our reality will become more discernible.

71. Are more angels present on Earth today than at any other time in history?

Yes. This is a result of free-will decisions that have called upon this realm to assist and guide, and to make adjustments. This has been unintentional in the minds of the small and on purpose in the minds of the great. The minds of the small are those who are deeply caught up in materiality. Through the desperate actions and greed of the small-minded, much harm has come to life on your home or planet. In these choices, there is an unconscious call for assistance from our realm. The greater minds represent those who are awakening, and these souls consciously perceive the need for healing. These souls call upon us with joy. This is a time that, if there were not divine intervention, those choices being made would have far-reaching consequences, affecting all universes.

72. Does the Human Kingdom evolve into the Angelic Kingdom?

It can happen sometimes. This depends on the will and life purpose of the individual soul. It is true that some members of the Human Kingdom are infused with angelic DNA through development of the divine tapestry. The purpose is to strengthen the unfolding plan on Earth.

73. Explain the difference between an angel and an archangel.

Your question would be likened to this: what is the difference between a human who is called a plumber and one who is called a senator? It is all in the job description. We would say to you that archangels have attributes, as do angels. The archangels are connected to the purpose that holds the patterning for the larger universal comings and goings:

Michael clears the pathway home and, in this purpose, has, in companionship with other angels, created the blueprint through which this path will remain accessible to all.

Gabriel organizes angels who work with individual life forms and holds the pattern for form. That is the abundance of possibilities, all of which are "on file" in the realm of Gabriel.

Raphael is the one who holds the pattern of perfection. This is why this one is called the "healing one." That is to say, this one, Raphael, in cooperation with other angels, restores the balanced state.

Uriel holds the pattern of manifestation, as created through the free-will choice of all beings, and weaves these into the divine tapestry.

All of these four archangels work in perfect harmony with angels who are in alignment with these assignments. None is greater or lesser than another.

Section Three

*

How We Met
the Angels

Chapter Seven

Ray and the
Angel of Truth

I have had many meaningful dreams throughout my life, the first appearing when I was five years old. In it, I was lifted into a heavenly temple filled with angels. Inside, every object seemed to radiate with a mysterious inner light. Beautiful, ethereal music played in the background, and it sounded so lovely; I was entranced. The mysterious beauty of the scene is difficult to describe in words, and yet the setting remains vivid to this day. What stood out most was the presence of angels. Although I could not discern specifically what these glorious beings were doing, they seemed to be quite busy throughout the temple. One guided me over to a golden platform where I saw my grandfather lying in peaceful repose. The angel spoke: "One day, your grandfather will give up his earthly body, and when this happens, it will mark a very important turning point in your life, for you will then embark upon a journey which will lead to the fulfillment of your mission on Earth." She continued on, saying that when this event occurred, my grandfather and the angels would guide me from this heavenly temple. The angel then told me that I would always remember this message, and that it would comfort me throughout my life. This was a profound experience for a five-year-old child, and even now, when I ponder the dream, I am silently in awe of the memory.

My grandfather died in 1982, the same year my daughter Kelly was born. Just as the dream foretold, that year marked the beginning of a profound adventure, although it wasn't exactly what I had in mind. Two weeks before Kelly's birth, I dreamed I went to an animal shelter to pick up my baby. She was a little lamb, with a satiny pink bow around her neck. I took her in my arms, and as I did, I heard someone speak: "This lamb is ill and will require a lot of attention. Wouldn't you like to choose a more healthy one?" "No," I replied. "This is the one for me." I remember feeling peaceful in the dream. Whoever had spoken to me indicated that I had made the perfect decision and wished me well. I awakened, wondering if my baby would be healthy. In contemplating the past, I feel that the being speaking to me in the dream was an angel. Even before her birth, the angels were on the scene.

After an unusually simple birth, I was deeply relieved when Kelly received a perfect ten on the Apgar, a test that measures the health of a newborn. Yet, a month later, I looked at her dear little face, and noticed her skin had a strange yellow hue. I promptly made an appointment with her pediatrician. After many tests and much waiting, the diagnosis was given. Kelly had a rare genetic disease called alpha-one anti-tripsin deficiency—a condition that causes a progressive cirrhosis of the liver in children. Eventually her liver would fail and she would need a liver transplant or she would die. She was given two years to reach this critical juncture. I felt my world rapidly coming apart. The idea of having a deathly ill child to care for ripped open my heart, and the pain and inability to cope led me into therapy.

While learning to deal with this crisis, I investigated and learned to use alternative healing methods to heal both my daughter and myself. While at the time these methods seemed to help, there were no guarantees. At some point, I knew I would have to "let go and let God," for ultimately *I* could not control whether she lived or died. It was during this time that I decided that, no matter what the outcome, I would focus on discovering a deeper meaning for Kelly's disease, and somehow find a way to allow the experience to enrich both our lives. Furthermore I wanted to share what I learned with others. This intention kept me from drowning in a sea of despair.

Adding to the stress of the situation, Kelly's father and I had divorced, and it had become necessary for her to live with him. His career eventually took them to Florida, six hundred miles away from me. Even though Kelly and I communicated by phone almost daily, and visited each other as often as possible, it was extremely difficult to accept the physical distance between us. I longed to ease her pain and suffering, and to hold her in my arms and nurture her.

Even though Kelly survived longer with her condition than the doctor originally predicted, by September 1994 her health was noticeably deteriorating, and we knew time was running out. She had been on a liver transplant list for eight months, but there was no news of a donor. One night, as we were talking, she said out of the blue, "Mom. I can feel my body getting weaker, and don't think I can hold on much longer. I saw a program on TV where angels helped another little girl who was sick get ready for her death, and I feel that they could help me, too. I'm really scared and I want to talk with angels, so they can help me get prepared. Can you help me learn how? Please?" Swirling emotions stirred in me as I listened to her words. I did not want my child to die. It was truly heart-wrenching. That night, for Kelly, I reached out to angels who might help, with an intensity and power I didn't know I had. I fell asleep feeling that Kelly's life and my own were about to change radically.

Early the next morning, I awoke with a vision in my mind's eye. I saw a board game through which people could directly communicate with angels. A family was sitting around the game, laughing and playing and having fun. Somehow, I "knew" immediately that this game was something I had to bring into being. I shared the scene with my husband, Larry, who immediately agreed to help me, and felt excited at the prospect of creating something that would help my beloved Kelly.

After the vision occurred, I naturally began thinking about angels more often, and recalled other encounters I had had with the Angelic Kingdom. Although my experiences were noteworthy, I humbly realized I was entering into the creation of *The Angels Talk* with very little real knowledge of the subject of angels. In fact, the only material I had ever read on the topic was Thomas and Deborah's book, *Angels: The Lifting of the Veil*. The book opened my eyes to a new and refreshing approach to the Angelic Kingdom. Previously I had considered angels as some kind of "milk-toast ethereal beings" who existed in another dimension; sometimes they touched our lives, but mostly not. Despite my personal experiences, I had never really considered that one could communicate with these beings on purpose until now. On the morning of my vision, I felt compelled to call Deborah and Thomas. I found myself blurting out an invitation for them to join Larry and me in creating the game. They agreed, and in September we met to lay out a plan.

One month into designing *The Angels Talk,* Kelly came to me with a question that took the wind right out of my sails: "Mom, do you think this game is really going to work?"

My heart quickened. "What do you mean?"

She repeated her question. "Do you really think the angels are going to come through this game and talk with us?"

Suddenly I realized that despite twenty-five years of an almost obsessive focus on spiritual studies, I still had doubts. Kelly had asked a question that triggered a number of my own. There was no way the game was going to work without the angels. What if they didn't want it to work? Or what if my vision was just a figment of an overactive imagination? What had I gotten us into? I had no choice but to move forward. I was compelled to find out the truth. More than anything, I wanted the game to work; I wanted the angels to talk with us, to teach us, and to open our hearts and minds. I also suspected that if *The Angels Talk* worked, my own doubts would be healed.

But there was more emotional pressure. In November, my mother, my greatest source of support with Kelly, underwent surgery to remove her gall bladder. When I was called and told that, during the operation, she was diagnosed with terminal cancer, I remember sobbing and screaming at God, while Larry held me in his arms. I cried for my mother, my daughter, myself, and my entire family, who had all been through so much emotional upheaval in the past eighteen months. Just a year and a half before, my beloved brother, Griff, and sister-in-law, Julie, had lost their five-year-old son in a tragic accident. They had, in their deepest moment of grief, offered my daughter their son's liver, but for medical reasons, we could not use my nephew's organ. Although heartbreaking, Griff and Julie's gift of love was extraordinary, and I was filled with unspeakable gratitude. As a result of this tragedy, my family had become closer and more unconditionally loving and supportive of one another. We were just beginning to peep over the edge of grief, when Kelly's and my mother's health began to decline more rapidly. Sometimes, when we're at the end of our ropes, there is nothing to do but let go. So, I did.

Still, there were three redeeming graces during those dark winter months. The first was my beloved husband, whose unwavering unconditional love and support were truly a godsend. The second saving grace was my twenty-three-year-old son, Rick, who came to live with us for four months, bringing laughter and joy into our home. Third, and not least, were the angels.

We had completed our prototype of *The Angels Talk,* and it worked better than I had expected. As the angels taught me how to communicate with them in an intimate way, I became stronger and more self-confident in my spiritual faith and in approaching the future with balance and grace. Not only did the game work, the angels continually comforted and assisted me in other ways—with signs and omens and miracles of love, light, and joy throughout my heavy-hearted winter. As for Kelly, the angels spelled out to her that she would receive a new organ by April. Kelly had complete and total faith that the angels had given her the truth. Honestly, I had some doubts, because I knew we were deeply attached to the answer we wanted to hear, and I was aware that emotional attachments can sometimes distort the angels' subtle communications.

In February, Kelly took a turn for the worse and was forced to remain on oxygen twenty-four hours a day. Thinking he might never see her again, Rick traveled to visit her one month later. One night while he was gone, Larry and I decided to spend a quiet night together and retire early. Around midnight, we were awakened by my brother pounding on our bedroom window, screaming for us to wake up. We ran to the front door. "The doctors have a liver for Kelly! She and her dad are on their way to the airport! She wants to talk with you before they board the plane." Minutes later, I was talking with Kelly. She felt afraid. After listening and responding to her fears, I reminded her to call on the angels and promised that Larry and I would soon be with her.

During the fourteen-hour drive to Cincinnati Children's Hospital Medical Center, where the transplantation would take place, I was in a state of shock. It was the longest fourteen hours of my life. I prayed during the entire trip, remembering all the years of waiting for this very moment. At times, tears would roll down my cheeks. As we arrived at the edge of the city, I saw a light out of the corner of my eye. I turned and saw a globe of golden light in the backseat! I was filled with hope and love. When it faded, I turned my attention to the road ahead and noticed something else. At first, I thought it was a large silvery cloud. But when it suddenly moved rapidly in the direction of the hospital, I noticed it had wings. The angels were with us.

Kelly came through the surgery like a trooper, with great courage and spunk. At one point while talking with the hospital chaplain, another angelic experience occurred. Larry and I were telling him how we had thought she wasn't going to live long enough to get her transplant. After all, she had been on the transplant list for fourteen months. The chaplain spoke: "You just never know about these things. Perhaps this is a miracle." No sooner had he spoken than the water in a nearby sink came pouring out of the faucet, full force! The three of us stared openmouthed.

Unfortunately I was not able to stay in Cincinnati more than a few days. However, her father stayed for the seven-week recuperation period, and we all felt blessed that one parent could be with her. Just before she was to fly home, she called and told me a story. When she was leaving the hospital, she looked up and saw three clouds in the distinct shape of giant angels in the sky. She felt truly comforted by the experience.

As for me, I had come full circle. I had traveled a very difficult path during the previous twelve years. True to the intention I had set when Kelly first became ill, I had found a deeper meaning, a gift, in the experience, and that gift was a profound sense of connection with the angels and the One-Who-Created-Us-All. I also knew that the time had come to share this gift with others. But how? At once, it occurred to me, I was already doing it! I was co-creating *The Angels Talk*.

Throughout that dark-night-of-the-soul winter, and then again in the spring, Deborah, Thomas, Larry, and I had been steadily playing the game. My ability to trust that we were truly communicating with the angels grew stronger with each passing session. As a result, I began to notice specific shifts in my outlook on life: I felt happier and more at peace than ever before, in spite of the obvious stress I was under. Angelic encounters were taking place on a daily basis, and it had become impossible not to believe in the magical and sacred world of these incredible light beings. By spring, an-other miracle occurred. My mother was sent home from the nursing home to recuperate, told by her doctors that she could possibly live many more years. Our lives had become a constant flow of miracles.

One day, the angels gave the four of us specific attributes or qualities to embody and embrace in order to complete the game and, as we learned, to discover the nature of our true selves. When I first saw them spell out "T-R-U-T-H" as my attribute, I was pleased. It resonated with my innermost being because, as far back as I could remember, there was nothing more I yearned for than truth itself. I had read literally thousands of books about all kinds of philosophies, cultures, and religions, seeking to find a simple truth that I could apply to any situation in my life. With this assignment came the hope that I would finally discover the "truth about truth." Yet my feelings of optimism were short-lived; they were followed by anxiety. The spiritual doubts that had arisen earlier were again haunting me. After all these years, it seemed I had not come very far in my desire to know what is truth. Now I was being called upon to embody, embrace, and experience truth. I knew I would have to have an unwavering focus and an abundance of angelic assistance in order to fulfill my task.

As I concentrated on my assignment, I couldn't help remembering my lifelong pursuit of truth. It wouldn't be long before I found what it was I was searching for. One day, while playing *The Angels Talk,* I asked the angels, "What is the most important message you would have us know?" I felt an incredible outpouring of energy as the angels spelled out their answer, and in it I found my own. The angels had responded, "*W-E A-R-E A-L-L O-N-E!*"

The next day, while meditating, I slipped into a vision. I was standing with the angels on a mountain, high above a meadow. They pointed toward some distant peaks, drenched in glistening blues, whites, and purples. A beautiful setting sun displayed an array of contrasting colors across the sky. I instantly became absorbed into a feeling of profound bliss, whereupon my entire being was completely and wholly enraptured by Truth itself. In that indescribable moment, *all* my questions were answered.

The next time we played *The Angels Talk,* the angels spelled out the next step in my assignment. They told me, "*Integrate truth with your concept of time.*" It took me a while to understand their message. Finally I understood that I needed to learn how to *apply* my mountaintop experience to my daily life, to my *time.* Over the months, I began to notice subtle changes. I was thinking more positively. I was more balanced emotionally. My internal attitude became one of gratitude. I began to take better care of my body. I became more prosperous. My relationships with others seemed easier and more rewarding than ever before, and I felt poised, confident, and peaceful in being able to handle whatever I was being given.

By playing *The Angels Talk* and following the angels' instructions, I have discovered an inner ability to make friends with my own personal attribute of truth, and to live my life more fully as a result. Through this miraculous gift, I have also realized success in accomplishing what I had originally intended to do: to help my daughter. Not only did we both learn how to communicate with the angels, I am personally convinced beyond a shadow of a doubt that angels played a large part in saving my child's life! I know now that we can communicate with the angels at will, *anytime, anyplace, anywhere,* and that they are willing to assist us with *anything.* There is only one requirement: we need to ask. And when we do, they *always* come!

Chapter Eight

Larry and the
Angel of Simplicity

$\mathcal{I}$ have been a seeker of personal and spiritual growth, and have sought explanations to the so-called mysterious things in life, for more than twenty years. This interest in all things "spiritual" took me on a journey in which I would find what I believed to be one truth, only to discover another equal but opposite one. Yet throughout my search, one desire stood out from all the rest: the desire to hear the voice of spiritual beings speaking to me directly. Granted, they did speak to me in various ways over the years. The problem was I didn't *hear* them, mainly because I believed heavenly voices had to come from out of the sky, instantly answering my every question, while bathing me in beams of light. Of course, this belief limited much of my ability to recognize the countless types of messages and information from the spiritual realm that I was actually receiving. So there I was, unable to see the proverbial forest for the trees, and all the while denying the richness of my experience.

Over the years, my curiosity netted what I consider some pretty "far-out" experiences, which opened the doors to realms of spirit I had never dreamed possible. I studied powerful masters like Don Juan Matus of Carlos Castaneda's fame, Seth, Lazarus, and a host of other well-intentioned souls who were popular back in the 1960s and 1970s. What's more, I had the great privilege to have many encounters with spiritual beings or entities in channeling sessions, which changed my life and educated me on concepts such as the flow of energy through the body, mind, emotions, and spirit. I learned to become aware of my daily, moment-to-moment intentions—or in some cases, the lack thereof—which helped me see clearly the importance of setting my intentions in life.

I met Kay in June 1988. Finally I had found my "twin soul" and a springboard into a higher understanding of the spiritual world. Within the first few hours of our meeting, we discovered that we had so much in common—I knew we were destined for each other. Our life stories were so similar, they could have been written by the same person. Suddenly my pursuit of spiritual ideas and experiences became even more joyful. Although, before meeting Kay, this path was a full and rich one and had offered much in the way of spiritual growth, I wouldn't have called any of my experiences "angelic" in nature. Kay would change all that.

The door to my awareness of the Angelic Kingdom opened when, one morning, Kay announced to me her vision. "Larry, I saw a family sitting at a table with a game board, and they were talking with angels. What would happen if you and I were to create a game for Kelly so she can learn to talk with her angels?" "Great," I thought to myself, "and how are we supposed to teach Kelly to talk with the angels, when I don't have the foggiest notion of how to talk with one—much less hear one!" Then a sobering thought occurred to me. If we were going to pull this off successfully, I would have to learn to communicate with the angels as soon as possible. Despite some resistance, I accepted the challenge.

I had always believed in angels and was attracted to paintings and pictures of angels—beautiful beings with wings and long flowing gowns, or pudgy little cupids with bows and arrows. I even prayed for an angel to appear to me once after reading several stories of angels making contact with humans. But, as for actually talking with angels, I figured conversation with heavenly beings was out of my reach. I would probably have to wait until I died, or else was involved in a life-threatening incident to bring on a visitation from angels. What I didn't know, as Kay spoke to me, was that the angels had already prepared some very interesting lessons for me and the others.

The angelic lessons began at the outset, when Kay invited two partners to join us in the project. Before I could give it another thought, *The Angels Talk* was under way. Initially, I'll admit, I was not very excited about having partners. I had definite feelings of foreboding and resistance to the idea. Aside from the fact that Deborah and Thomas had just completed their book on angels, I grumbled to myself that I didn't understand why the angels had put the four of us together. After all, I hardly knew Deborah and Thomas.

Despite my concerns, we set to work. Since I have a background in graphic arts, I set out to design the prototype game board. The four of us met several times to work on the project, and each meeting involved several lengthy discussions. In the past, I had not been one to speak my mind in a group situation. But, for some strange reason, I suddenly found myself expressing my opinions strongly. The truth is, it even surprised me. I had not experienced this side of myself before—certainly not such conviction. In fact, when someone disagreed with me, it was as if I was being asked to give up everything I owned instead of simply trying to agree on a game. I have to confess, I also held many judgments about my new partners—which only added fuel to the smoldering fire of resentment inside me. Still, we carried on, although, as Thomas once said, we might have referred to ourselves as the "angel group from hell."

Three months after we began, our negative opinions of each other reached a peak. In each of our weekly sessions, at least one of us could expect to end up on the "chopping block" for one foible or another. By the end of each meeting, however, we learned to heal the discord so that we felt like friends again. We were all in agreement on one sure thing, the One-Who-Created-Us-All was definitely in charge. We were slowly learning the process of cooperation. My commitment to the project helped me persevere, and strangely enough, this process helped me learn to speak up. By doing so, I began to trust myself more and believe that I had something of value to say—that my thoughts and feelings counted, not just in the group but in the larger scheme of things as well. A new self-confidence was emerging, and I liked what I was learning about myself. I realize now, looking back, that going through that process was another angelic lesson. They were helping all of us purge ourselves of unwanted habits, ideas, notions, and belief systems about ourselves and each other.

By the end of December, we had completed the prototype game board and were having weekly sessions with the angels. I was elated—it actually worked! We were able to receive messages from the unseen world. Was my dream really coming true? It was. They told us they were pleased we had taken the opportunity to commune with them, and if we agreed, they would help us build a bridge between the

Angelic and Human Kingdoms. From that moment forward, my judgments and resistance began to melt. Gradually, as I played the game, I began to apply the angels' most repeated concept—We Are All One.

Early in the next year, Deborah was elected to go to New York to meet our agent and find a publisher for the game. Our spirits were high when she called to tell us that our game was met with great enthusiasm by various publishers. Unfortunately her good news turned out to be double-edged. Although the publishers liked the game, they wanted us to write a companion book. I did not want to write a book and, in truth, harbored feelings of inadequacy about writing. I simply wanted to give the game to a publisher and return with Kay to our simple lives. What's more, I didn't see how the four of us could ever write a book together, when trying to agree with one another had often been so difficult.

The angels, however, wanted a book—and told us they would help write it. In fact, they spelled out an outline and assigned different chapters for the four of us to write. Given that level of commitment from the angels, I saw the wisdom in continuing with the project. It would be challenging, but I wondered if it might not be fun doing it. By early March, three months after a publisher had tentatively agreed to buy it, we heard from our agent: Penguin definitely wanted the project. By this time, with the angels' help, the four of us were getting closer. As our weekly sessions with the angels continued, I began experiencing more joy. Then the real work began.

On April 19, 1995, I was given a most important task: to embody the attribute of simplicity. Although I didn't know exactly what this meant, I agreed immediately. I questioned why I was chosen for the attribute of simplicity. After all, I thought my life was fairly simple already. Feeling confused, I asked the angels for an explanation. They spoke through the board and said, ". . . *you would do well to translate this attribute into your experience and notice how simplicity changes your perspective on a practical level.*" One of the ways the angels suggested this task could be made easier was to pretend that I was the Angel of Simplicity, and to look at myself and the world from its perspective. Also, each day I was to ask myself, "What have I done to embody my attribute today?" and "How have I supported the others in their attributes?" I tried looking at my world through the eyes of the Angel of Simplicity, but it didn't work at first. In fact, I discovered—through trial and error—that simple activities such as going to the grocery store, working with my computer, or mowing the lawn all had the potential to entangle me in a world of complications. I gave the concept of simplicity endless thought and reread the transcripts from several sessions with the angels to gain more insight. I was sure of one thing. Whatever project I undertook, no matter how small or large, it suddenly seemed filled with complications of all sorts. This was, as you might guess, very frustrating, and only one of the many incidents that occurred. What was I doing wrong? Whatever this simplicity thing was, I had clearly not gotten the message. A month passed and still no clarity on my assigned attribute. I was determined to understand simplicity, so I prayed for the angels' continuing assistance.

One night I dreamed of my Guardian Angel, Proseriel. Although this dream was a direct communication from the Angelic Kingdom, it did not answer my questions about simplicity. I felt like a simpleton, a dunce. Why was I so slow at grasping something that could be so simple! Despite all my confusion, there was one saving grace: playing the game. It helped to familiarize and establish, within my physical senses, the feeling of Spirit flowing through me. With practice, I discovered it well within my ability to feel this flow in my daily life. Part of this newly discovered awareness was simply listening to my body.

The angels explained that the body is a transmitter and receptor of information and communications from Spirit, or the One. I began to ask myself what my body felt at any given moment: was I thirsty, tired, hungry, happy, angry, sore? Did I feel resistant, compassionate, or joyful? Could I feel Spirit in whatever action I was about to undertake? All the feelings and sensations in my body were supposed to mean something. If I took the time to listen carefully to my body, the angels said it would give me clues as to what to do. For example, if I felt pressure in my throat while listening to someone speak, it would mean that I had a response I needed to verbalize. I was being asked to express my perceptions and my truth, and I was slowly beginning to listen.

The turning point for me came when I bought a new computer program, to make things simpler—I thought. My body and other signs pointed out to me to wait, but I ignored them. Installing the new program succeeded in preventing several of my older programs from running at all. It took at least three days to clean up the damage. This was my coup de grâce in my search for simplicity. This last experience of complication really got my attention. I had received information from my body and ignored it. I finally understood that I really needed to "listen" to my body and my intuition to discern what the One-Who-Created-Us-All was trying to tell me and, better yet, to apply what I was "hearing." Over the next few days my awareness grew. I listened carefully to my body and the feelings inside. I began consulting it about every decision, no matter how simple. I felt as if I was in the flow, in the right place at the right time, free from doubt. Although the messages were subtle, as it turned out, I *was* communicating with heavenly beings, or Spirit, through my body. This was my simplicity. These messages were an answer to my long-held desire to communicate with heavenly beings. After decades of searching "out there," the answers were within me all along—simplicity. "How beautiful," I thought, "and how simple a way to talk with the One." Understanding my attribute of simplicity was finally flowing through into my consciousness.

I also had another revelation. I was looking back through the transcripts from a game session in June. In that session, the angels had suggested, "*Do not attempt to separate your lessons. It is the same, even with its seeming nuances of difference. Each one of you has been called to shift your awareness . . . you stand at the precipice of manifestation, or action, or the bringing of* (each of our attributes) *into your daily experience.*" I suddenly realized that I had not been alone in my struggle to understand my attribute of simplicity. My wife and partners had also been challenged as they struggled to understand their attributes. This idea gave new meaning to the phrase "We Are All One!" By a strange coincidence, at our next meeting, we had all come to the same understanding: the angels say that by listening to our inner senses we are "aligning with the One"—how simple! After all those months of struggle with what appeared to be complicated lessons from the angels, I finally came to see simplicity in all I encounter. It's so easy!

The experience of creating the game and writing this book changed my life forever. Creating an alliance with the angels and, eventually, embodying my attribute of simplicity has proved not only to be a great joy, but a valuable learning experience and an answer to my prayers of the last twenty years.

Chapter Nine

Deborah and the Angel of Beauty

I was five when I saw my first angel. Lying in bed asleep, I was startled awake by a flash of light. When I opened my eyes, there it was, hovering above me, in a shimmering cloud of the most beautiful colors I had ever seen. This wouldn't be my only encounter with angels. There were others. When my family moved to the mountains, I would roam the hills and woods and escape deep into the forest where I was certain no one could find me. I would lie there for hours and watch the tiny angels peeking out from the thickets, calling me to play. Often I would follow them and they would take me on journeys down the paths the hunters left, up one ridge and down another, and we would talk mind-to-mind.

Finally, exhausted with the angels' game of hide-and-seek, I would flop down in the tall grass and listen for a voice I secretly called "God." He would tell me things that made sense of my life and I would feel peaceful and loved in a way I never felt in the world. But when dusk came and the forest filled with shadows and I returned home, the voice would go quiet and I would escape to my room, confused and strangely alone.

As the years flew by, I became convinced that something was dreadfully wrong with me. Other people seemed content with their lives. Was it my world of angels and voices that made "real life" so painful? I began to think so, and by the time I had reached my twenties, I had convinced myself my experiences were all just wishful thinking. The little girl who once believed in invisible things went underground, and I looked to the "real world" to find some way to survive. Increasingly confused, I began to think that maybe marriage or a child or some gorgeous mansion in the woods would make me happy. They didn't; nothing did. Over the years, everything I wished for came true. I married twice, had a son, beautiful homes, and money to spare, yet none of it gave me the peace I craved.

By my early thirties, I could ignore it no longer. I would have to find some semblance of peace or simply go mad. So, one fateful night, alone and on my knees, I called out to the one comfort I had ever known—the voice and the angels—and begged them to return. One week later, I left my husband, packed my eight-year-old son off to live with my mother, and rented a house on the beach. Alone and terrified, I again called out to the angels, to help me learn to write. They answered my call. Two days later, on a hunch, I called the editor of a local health magazine, hoping he might take a chance and offer me an assignment. To my surprise, he asked me to meet him the very next day. After telling him my story, he closed his eyes for a few moments and when he opened them, smiling mysteriously, he offered me his job. He was preparing to move to the mountains and had been praying for someone to take his place. Something told him that that someone was me.

I took the job and loved it. But my happiness was short-lived. One year later, the job ended suddenly, and once again, I was thrown into uncertainty. I applied for any job I could to pay the bills, but no one would hire me. Gradually, over the next two months, I began to experience an exhaustion that made even the simplest movement nearly impossible. Eventually, in desperation, I consulted a psychic. She told me I needed to write a book, many books, in fact, and that my illness was simply the cry of a soul that knew no other way to get my attention. To this day, I can still hear her final words ringing in my ears: "Call on the angels for help. They are waiting to assist you in the work."

The next morning, I dragged the typewriter into my bed and stepped across the threshold into the world of my imagination, where once again angels spoke to me, mind-to-mind, and I wrote. Within a year, I had completed my first novel. But when I sent it out, not a single publisher showed the slightest interest. As the rejection letters piled up, and I attempted to make a living as a freelance writer, I stepped into a period of turmoil that lasted nearly ten years. Later I would look back on this time in wonder at how blessed I had been to experience an apprenticeship with angels. But at the time, I simply thought I was a failure and there was nothing I could do to change it.

By the spring of 1992, life had become easier, and once again I found myself dreaming of writing a book. Then one unusually warm day in April, while browsing in a local bookstore, I happened upon a rack of angel books. Goose bumps went up and down my spine and I suddenly "knew" it was time to tell the story of my own journey with the Angelic Realm. When I returned home, I felt strangely compelled to call Thomas, who I knew taught angel workshops, to join me in the writing of the book. Though I didn't know it at the time, he had been trying to write his own angel book for years, and just the day before had been down on his knees asking the angels for help. Within a few short months, we had a publisher, and one year later our book, *Angels: The Lifting of the Veil,* was completed.

Within a week, I received an offer to move to a tiny trailer in the woods on the outskirts of Virginia Beach. In retrospect, it was clearly a "divine setup." As the summer progressed, I found myself letting go of all the previous years of chaos. No car, penniless, there was nothing left but the exquisite beauty of nature just beyond my porch stoop. Often I would laugh at the absurdity of it; after all my gorgeous homes, here I was with a few motley possessions, in a tiny tin trailer in the middle of nowhere, and I was happier than I had ever been.

It was during this period that I received Kay's call about the angel game. At the time, I was not particularly excited at the prospect of leaving the blissful solitude of my woods. Yet the gnawing sense that I might be turning away from something important grew stronger by the moment. Finally, in late September, I agreed to join the group. Today I thank God I listened to the urging of that inner voice, because it was an experience that would change my life forever.

When we began to play the game on a weekly basis, the door opened to a closeness with the Angelic Realm that I had never dreamed possible. *"Consider that you have the ability to sit down with us in the flesh and talk normally. What would you want to know about us?"* they asked. And so we did, for hours on end, asking every question imaginable, from the silliest—How many angels fit on the end of a pin?—to the most personal and profound. Although, at the time, I didn't doubt that angels were real, this was a whole new level of intimacy, which I had never experienced with another dimension. With each question answered, I began to catch a glimpse of just how awesome these invisible beings actually are. Formless and free, they seem to dance through life in a constant state of joy. And in contrast to our human world of worry and concern, to them life is miraculous—a constant experience of love.

Granted, their notion that it was possible to learn without suffering was a little unfathomable in the beginning. *"When you stop struggling,"* they said, *"and let the feeling of Oneness with all things fill you, you will begin to experience life as abundant joy."* "Could it really be that simple?" I'd wonder. I wanted to believe it was, yet in the day-to-day experience of mundane life, it continued to escape me. Although I had always longed to feel that oneness, when I did, it was only for moments. Each time, I'd return to feeling separate and alone. But as the days flew by, the noble idea of Oneness was finally becoming a reality. How could it not, in the presence of beings who knew nothing else? Much to my surprise, life was getting easier, and it was a whole new experience.

But the real change began when we received our celestial homework assignment. Each of us was given a specific angel or group of angels that expressed a certain attribute of God. Our task was to call upon them constantly and get to know them so well we could actually experience the world as if we were looking at it through their eyes. I was assigned the Angel of Beauty and told, *"Pay attention to this attribute and all the ways it occurs naturally in your life."*

For months on end, I threw myself into the study of

beauty. I searched through books and mentally reviewed the events of my past to try to discover where I had seen it and what it looked like when I did. It forced me to come face-to-face with the little girl inside me who believed something about her was dreadfully wrong. But this time, instead of seeing what was wrong, I saw her innocence and beauty and the intimacy she had once had with invisible things.

Over the next few months, I began to notice the many miracles of everyday life all around me. When I needed a quiet place to live, a beautiful apartment, one that I would grow to love, miraculously opened up in Kay and Larry's backyard. When I prayed for work that would give me time to write, it appeared. Friends showered me with love and kindness. Had it always been this way, or was I seeing my life through new eyes?

Then, one particularly gorgeous day in October, a little more than a year after the project had begun, it all made sense. I was alone in the woods at the time, propped up against a tree, when I bolted up in amazement. In one glorious instant, the events of my life arranged themselves into an exquisitely beautiful pattern. "Of course," I whispered. "How brilliant that *I* had been given the assignment of beauty." Up until my trailer days, I had experienced most of my life as painful; but now I saw that the pain had been my choice. I had *chosen* to turn away from the beauty and miracle of ordinary life—and it happened when I turned away from the beauty and innocence of the little girl inside. At that moment, she peeked out from where she had been hiding deep inside, and all the way home, tiny angels appeared to me, just as they had a long time ago.

Chapter Ten

Thomas and the Angel of Purification

I have always believed that there is a God, a Source who loves us just as we are, without judgment or conditions. It has been my personal quest to discover this God and, in so doing, create an intimate relationship that would last for eternity.

Despite a very challenging and often difficult life, this quest has remained foremost in my mind and heart, giving me the determination to keep going despite many personal defeats. Growing up in Ohio, school, both elementary and junior high, was a nightmare. Despite real efforts to try to do well, I simply couldn't and failed the first, third, fifth, and eighth grades. Eventually I dropped out, certain that I was stupid. In 1968, with no other options, I joined the army. Although I enjoyed it and, much to my parents' surprise, excelled, even academically, when I was discharged in 1971, I was faced with a difficult challenge. During my military experience, I found it easier to deal with my self-defeating beliefs about myself by using drugs and alcohol. While this made me feel better for a while, eventually it simply made my self-esteem only worse. So, in an attempt to find help, I joined a metaphysical study group led by a most wonderful woman who would become my first real teacher in my quest to find my God. Her name was Flo-Bird. She taught me to pray and meditate, and tried her best to show me the wisdom of loving myself, since, as she often said, self-love is a necessary prerequisite to discovering God. Unfortunately, at the time, I didn't fully grasp the idea and so continued my quest, assuming I could somehow bypass that step.

In 1974, I met the woman of my dreams, and we were married one year later. The minister who officiated at the wedding was a man named Paul Solomon, the founder of The Fellowship of the Inner Light, a nondenominational church. Its teachings are based on the belief that truth and joy are at the core of all religions, and that expressing them is the highest form of worship. I was so impressed with Paul's relationship with God that I decided to study to become a minister. It was in 1991, while enrolled in the Fellowship's seminary program in New Market, Virginia, that I discovered the Angelic Kingdom. At the time, we were learning new meditation techniques, and I found, much to my surprise, that whenever I became quiet and still, angels would gather around me. When I asked, "Why are you here?" they would respond instantly with this one loving phrase: "*Dearly Beloved: we come to assist you and answer your questions.*" After I got over my initial shock, I gradually began to learn to ask for their assistance as I went about my daily life. For instance, one day when I was in need of financial help and turned to the angels, their response was simple and clear: "*Ask and you shall receive.*" So I asked God for the income I needed and waited patiently until the next day, when I again prayed for help. This time, the angels responded with "*Dearest Thomas: You have already asked. Now have faith in your Source.*" The message came with such love I found myself mysteriously at peace. Sure enough, the next day, a card arrived in the mail with a check for one thousand dollars and a tiny badge that read, "*God Keeps His Promises.*"

Over the years, as my relationship with the angels grew more intimate, I discovered that not only did they answer my questions, they were always ready and willing to respond to my call. Whether I asked them to find a parking place or protect my teenage children, nothing was too big or too small for them. By the time I had concluded my seminary training in 1982, I was willingly calling the angels into almost every part of my life.

Upon graduation, I immediately entered into my life's work: lecturing and teaching personal growth and transformation seminars and angel workshops around the world. Everywhere I went, I always invoked angelic assistance, and the angels responded every time. In fact, during lectures, they would often tell me beforehand what questions or concerns were forming in the audience's minds as I spoke. When I trusted this guidance and responded accordingly, participants would often come to me later wondering how in the world I had anticipated their unspoken queries.

Yet, despite the fact that my relationship with the Angelic Kingdom continued to expand, there was one area of my life in which I was still disinclined to ask for assistance: my relationship with myself. I was more than willing to be of service to others. My problem was expressing the same love and caring toward Self. Although I naively assumed that my problem with Self would be healed by serving others, in truth I was my own worst enemy. Thomas needed my unconditional love, and I was not willing to give it. Intellectually I knew that my relationship with myself was the cornerstone of my life and the key to all other relationships, including my relationship with God, but healing it simply seemed like an impossible task.

In September 1994, my journey took a new turn when I received a phone call from Kay about her vision of an angel game. I knew instantly that it was a divine inspiration, and I could feel the presence of angels throughout our conversation. When she asked if I would be interested in joining in the co-creation of the game, I was thrilled and agreed without hesitation.

Deborah and I had recently finished writing a book on angels, and the experience had taught us much about angels, as well as about ourselves. So, the opportunity to work with the angels once again far outweighed the difficulties I knew might arise from working in a group experience of co-creation.

As the project unfolded, and we were each given our assignments, it did seem as if the angels had my personal quest in mind, particularly when they gave us our attributes. Initially I was overjoyed when I received the Angel of Purification, as purification was an obvious need in my life. Yet, as I delved deeper into the meaning of my attribute, I realized that embracing my attribute could be my worst nightmare, since it would force me to take a closer look at my beliefs and addictions and to deal with my relationship with myself—once and for all. While one part of me was eager to get on with the transformational process, another part was finding every excuse possible to avoid the whole experience. As it turned out, this time I would not be able to escape from learning the critical lesson of loving myself.

A year into creating *The Angels Talk,* my life began to change dramatically. First, in late August, I was asked to leave my position as Pastor and Director of the Virginia Beach Fellowship Church, as the board of directors was forced to eliminate my paid position. The very next week, MaryAnna, my wife of twenty years, decided she was ready to strike out on her own and informed me that she was leaving me. Our marriage was over. Although this was not what I wanted, I saw no way of preventing it. So, we separated lovingly, and she and our fifteen-year-old daughter, Tara, moved to Texas. Simultaneously, Timothy, our eighteen-year-old son, left home to live with a friend. Leaving me completely alone was clearly a "divine setup" for one who so desperately needed to deal with himself.

In the midst of the pain I was feeling over what was happening to my life, I turned to the angels. For the first time, I sincerely asked for help with myself. As always, they responded with unconditional love and assistance. Their first instruction was that I needed to focus on my unbearable pain and let it take me on "a journey of truth." Then, they continued, "*You must start a love affair with yourself.*" They even told me how: I was instructed to go into the woods and spend three days and three nights alone. On the first two days, I was to let go of everything: the feelings of loss, regret, guilt, self-doubt, everything. On the third day, I was to write down my intention concerning what I wanted my life to stand for, and to be willing to receive blessings from the One-Who-Created-Us-All. Finally the angels shared with me a most interesting concept. "*Dearest Thomas,*" they said, "*set down your pain and suffering. You have chosen to suffer long enough. Now choose peace and happiness, and start your journey home to the Kingdom.*" Could it be true that I didn't have to suffer, that I could learn to let go and to not be disappointed by the choices others made, even when they affected my life directly? When I looked at this closely, I discovered that my pain and suffering had no purpose, nor did it change anything other than my own well-being.

But there was another message, and this one helped the most. "*Dear One*," they said, "*learn to focus on the holy aspects in all things of the One and perceive life from this perspective, allowing it to be your reference. And, bless all things around you: everything, all people, all parts of yourself, and your shadow as well. After you have blessed all these things, send them into the Light-of-the-One.*"

Today I find myself a little stronger and a bit wiser as, every day, I love myself more. The Angels of Purification have become my loving companions, and I can only shake my head in amazement at all the wonderful ways the angels have guided me through this life-changing experience. As I learned to release all things, I discovered yet another truth: that which is in our best interest and is meant to be will return in God's time and with God's love. And so it was that MaryAnna and Tara eventually returned. The quest for a more intimate relationship with a God that loves me uncon-ditionally is not yet complete—perhaps it is never com-plete—yet I *know* now that my loving God lives within, so the search for something outside myself is over. As I reflect on the past year, and realize all that came about from one mother's heartfelt desire to help her blessed daughter, I can only bow my head and give thanks.

Chapter Eleven

The Spirit of Cooperation

Know, realize, understand, and have an awareness that you can absolutely retain your individual will and also fully cooperate, enmesh, connect, and bond with the will of others. In the end, everyone gets their own way, their own path fulfilled, and can further embrace the fact or truth that we are all One, living and co-creating within the grand design of Universal Will. All is according to Divine Plan. Drop your self-importance, all of you, and move forward with us and bask in the glory of the One-Who-Creates-Us-All. You will be called upon to continue to surrender your will to truth. Begin to perceive one another as the angels of your attributes and, as a whole, as angels of co-operation. We love you.

—THE ANGELS

$\mathcal{W}$hen Kay shared her vision of what was to become *The Angels Talk,* and we all agreed to come together to co-create it, a spiritual alliance was formed that included not just four human beings, but the entire Angelic Kingdom. Our intention was to create a game to help a child, who we thought at the time was dying, to talk with the angels. It wasn't until we had completed the prototype game board and actually had our first conversations with the angels that we became aware of their loving intentions. Together with the angels, we were asked to build what they called a "bridge" between the Human and Angelic Kingdoms, one that would be used by many people the world over to establish a relationship not only with the angels, but more importantly with the One-Who-Created-Us-All. By accepting this assignment we would aid in the realization of Heaven-on-Earth. Furthermore, if we chose to do so, the angels *promised* that our lives would be changed in ways we could barely imagine.

We weren't sure if their promise was a blessing or an omen! Yet the opportunity to work and play with the angels in this heavenly venture inspired us to move forward on the never-ending highway of possibilities that lay ahead.

The concept was easy enough to understand, yet building the bridge seemed an enormous and humbling task. What's more, the angels told us, in order to accomplish this task, there was one important requirement: we would have to experience the "true" spirit of cooperation, for cooperation would be the cornerstone of this bridge, the actual starting place on which all else would rest.

So, we set about our task, though we didn't pay much heed to the angels' message about cooperation. We thought cooperation simply meant working together, so why give it much thought? In truth, at the time, we simply didn't recognize the overall importance of it—as individuals or as a group. It wasn't until later, when the angels gave us the outline for the book, spelling out that the spirit of cooperation would be the subject of the last chapter, that we actually began to look for the true meaning of it. But the final chapter was far off in the future, and we assumed we would cross *that* bridge when we came to it.

We were so giddy with excitement and filled with passion by the angelic request that we set to work with what seemed like the bliss of newlyweds on their wedding night. However, in a short time, our "honeymoon" was over. One by one, our shadows began to emerge. We discovered only too quickly that we had differing opinions and understandings of what commitment to *The Angels Talk* meant. Judgments, doubts about ourselves and each other, and beliefs about working in groups arose. Paradoxically, as the shadows grew darker, our limited perceptual filters were brought into the light. Power struggles developed between us. No matter how hard we tried, we could not impose our individual wills upon one another. Eventually we came to an impasse and were just plain stuck! Fighting the raging battles within, we began to ignore each other and withdrew to question our intentions. We were indeed meeting our Selves.

The angels implored each of us to ask, "Would we just give lip service to the ideal of Oneness or truthfully walk our talk?" During this period of withdrawal and subsequent contemplation, we each became aware of the truth, simplicity, purity, and beauty of our hearts' desires. As we awakened to the love, and surrendered to it, there came the realization that we would do whatever it took to fulfill our agreement with each other, the angels, and the One-Who-Created-Us-All. Accepting an inner responsibility to cooperate became a joy. Out of our painful lessons came the profound gift of unconditional love.

As we worked together in joyous and cooperative waves

of intention, we could hear the angels of our attributes gently urging us along. The Angel of Truth urged us to be true to our hearts' desires and diligent in our intention to cooperate in love. The Angel of Beauty asked us to reach out and help one another gently, and to look for the beauty and wisdom in our experience. The Angel of Simplicity requested that we listen to the others, plot out what came next, step-by-step, and stay open to the possibilities that were ahead of us. The Angel of Purification suggested we purify our intentions and our lives on each and every level of beingness. We had to be willing to share our truth. As we embraced the spirit of cooperation, the pieces finally fell into place.

Through our collective efforts, as we worked closely with the angels and each other, slowly we came to understand and experience the nuances of cooperation. Everyone had an individual assignment that dovetailed into the group's and the angels' plans. We had found our way and were happy with the transformations that occurred within us. Looking back, though, we felt it would have been a lot easier if the angels had just told us the whole plan, all at once. Instead we received it one step at a time. The angels said that we humans have free will and due to the angels' patterning, they could not interfere with our lessons. We had to *choose* the spirit of cooperation for ourselves.

The angels were as intent on helping us understand the idea of cooperation as they were on getting *The Angels Talk* and their messages of love out into the world. When we finally felt the spirit of cooperation fully and completely, we were only weeks away from our deadline for completion of the manuscript. Suddenly we were so busy you could almost see the smoke rising from our fingertips as we sat at our computers and finally poured out our souls' intents.

Just as Adam and Eve came to the Garden of Eden with innocence, so too did our group come to *The Angels Talk* with the simple intention to joyfully create a child's game. There was no thought of consequences, and as one could expect, we encountered a strange duality. We explored the depths of our self-importance—the concept of separation—and fell from grace in our own eyes and in one another's as well. We crucified one another and ourselves for what seemed like differences, and within the process of our some-times painful initiation, we learned to surrender to the will of the One. We communed with angels, on the board and in our hearts, and discovered a brighter awareness of coopera-tion. Eventually, by applying the angels' constant and loving assistance to embody and embrace our attributes, and of course the "true" spirit of cooperation, we were brought into the light. The angels' *promise* came true.

Our bridge between the Human and Angelic Kingdom is now complete, and the heartfelt experience of Heaven-on-Earth is literally at our fingertips. What we have presented here is but a "shadow," if you will, of the overall impact the experience of cooperation had in our ever-evolving lives. Today we are so completely humbled by our relationship with the angels and the spirit of cooperation, not to men-tion each other, we can only guess at the totality of the lessons learned by all. As nearly as we can tell, it never ends; the completion of *The Angels Talk* is only the beginning!

It is our deepest and most heartfelt wish that you, too, may come to make the same journey across this bridge-between-worlds, and that you will choose to intimately commune with the angels, allowing the spirit of coopera-tion to fill your hearts and minds fully and completely. We love you.

—THE AUTHORS AND *ALL* THE ANGELS

The authors and inventors of *The Angels Talk* are deeply interested in your experiences with the angels and the game, and we invite you to share these with us by writing to the address below. Please include your name and address so we can share any new projects or information with you.

The Angels Talk
2100 Mediterranean Ave., Suite 42
Virginia Beach, VA 23451